The Graduation
of Jake Moon

Other books by Barbara Park

The Junie B. Jones series

Mick Harte Was Here
Dear God, Help!!! Love, Earl
Rosie Swanson: Fourth-Grade Geek for President
Maxie, Rosie, and Earl—Partners in Grime
My Mother Got Married (and Other Disasters)
Almost Starring Skinnybones
The Kid in the Red Jacket
Buddies
Beanpole
Operation: Dump the Chump
Skinnybones
Don't Make Me Smile

BARBARA PARK

The Graduation
of Jake Moon

An Anne Schwartz Book
ALADDIN PAPERBACKS
New York   London   Toronto   Sydney   Singapore

First Aladdin Paperbacks edition June 2002
Copyright © 2000 by Barbara Park

ALADDIN PAPERBACKS
An imprint of Simon & Schuster
Children's Publishing Division
1230 Avenue of the Americas
New York, NY 10020

Also available in an Atheneum Books for Young Readers hardcover edition.
Book design by Jim Hoover
The text of this book was set in Century School Book BT
Printed in the United States of America
14 16 18 20 19 17 15

The Library of Congress has cataloged the hardcover edition as follows:
Park, Barbara.
The graduation of Jake Moon / by Barbara Park.—1st ed.
p. cm.
Summary: Fourteen-year-old Jake recalls how he has spent the last four years of his life
watching his grandfather descend slowly but surely into the horrors of Alzheimer's
disease.
ISBN 0-689-83912-X (hc.)
[1. Alzheimer's disease—Fiction. 2. Grandfathers—Fiction.]
I. Title.
PZ7.P2197   Gr2000   [Fic]—dc21   99-87475
ISBN 0-689-83985-5 (Aladdin pbk.)

To the everyday heroes like Jake to whom life
has dealt a different set of cards
—B. P.

Contents

1

The Twist

There are these three eighth-grade boys. They've just gotten out of school for the day. And they're about to take off in different directions, when they notice something going on in the trash Dumpster at the other end of the parking lot.

They're still pretty far away from it, but they can see an old man sitting on the edge of the thing. His back is facing them, and he's just sort of balancing himself there. Staring down into the bottom of the Dumpster.

The boys watch him for a second. And then one of them starts grinning. And he cups his hands around his mouth and shouts out, "Hey! Don't jump, Pops! You've got everything to live for!"

Then one of the other boys yells, "Yeah! Plus I heard the food is much better at the Dumpster up the street!"

So after that, both kids totally crack up. And it becomes this contest, sort of, to see who can holler out the funniest insults at the old guy.

Like the first kid asks the old man if he went to *P.U. University*. And then the second kid asks if he has any *Grey Poupon*.

But the third kid, see, he's just standing there not saying a word. Instead, his eyes are glued to the old guy, almost. Like he's waiting for a reaction.

Only that's the thing. Because there *is* no reaction. Not at first, anyway. At first, the old man never even turns around. So the boys begin to think that maybe the guy's deaf or something. Which totally takes the fun out of shouting insults.

But then—out of the blue—something seems to click in the old man's brain. I mean, even from the back you can see his head sort of perk up. It's like he *gets* it now, you know? He suddenly understands that all this yelling has been directed at him.

And so he lowers himself down into the trash bin. And then he turns around to see who's been talking to him.

And that's pretty much that. The fun is over. Because even from the other end of the parking lot, it's obvious to the boys that there's something really wrong with the old guy. That he's just not right in the head. Instead of acting mad or angry or even insulted, his face actually brightens. And he waves as friendly as anything, and shouts, "Hullo, fellas!"

And it's so pathetic, I can't even tell you.

The two boys shut up after that. I mean, they chuckle a little bit and all. But you can tell they're not exactly busting with pride over making fun of a retarded old man.

But see, the *third* kid—the one who kept quiet—he doesn't have anything to be ashamed about at all. Because like I said, he didn't do anything.

So if you happened to be passing by and you saw this whole thing going on, you'd probably think that the third kid was the good kid. That he was the one with a conscience or some sense of decency or something.

Only that's the weird thing about this story.

That's the *twist,* I guess you'd call it.

On account of the third kid turned out to be the most shameful of all.

Because the third kid was me.

And the old man in the Dumpster was my grandfather.

2

Thor, God of Thunder

My name is Jake Moon.

No middle name.

And it's not Jacob.

It's just Jake. And it's just Moon. And I like it pretty well. Which isn't bragging. Because I had nothing to do with it at all.

My grandfather named me. And okay, I know that normally it's the parents who name the kid. But my mother wasn't exactly in a solid frame of mind when I was born. In fact, her thinking was so muddled she never even told my father she was going to have a baby.

Ma met him her third year in college. They went together for over a year, she said. And then, on the anniversary of their first date, he asked her out to dinner. He told her he had something really important to ask her that night. So she was positive he was going to give her an engagement ring.

That afternoon, she went to the bank and withdrew

enough money to get herself an expensive manicure. She told me that she wanted her hands to look "fashion magazine perfect" when he put the ring on her finger.

The trouble was, when my father came to pick her up, he was wearing cut-off jeans and a T-shirt. And instead of taking her to a big, fancy restaurant, he drove her to Arby's and ordered two Beef 'n' Cheddars.

Ma was still holding out hope, though. She said she almost fainted when they finally finished eating and he reached for her hand. Then he held it in his, real romantic and all. And he asked if he could please date her roommate.

The next day, my mother packed up everything she owned and drove to stay with a friend of hers in Connecticut. Three weeks after she got there, she found out I was on the way.

She didn't tell my grandfather. Not right away, I mean. My mother has always been the independent type, and she wanted to make sure she could support us before she let anyone know.

She made up all sorts of excuses not to go home to visit for all those months. She worked at Denny's right until the week I was born. And two weeks after that, she went right back to work again.

If I had been a normal baby, it might have turned out okay, too. But I was one of those mixed-up kinds of babies who cry all night and sleep all day. So after two solid weeks of listening to me scream, my mother was a walking bundle of raw nerves.

Unfortunately, on her first afternoon back at Denny's

some old woman started chewing her out pretty good because there was "a hair in her pie." It's one of those lessons in life we can all learn from, I think. Never complain about a hair in your pie when your waitress is teetering on the brink of insanity.

Ma picked up the plate, turned it over on the woman's head, and said, "What a coincidence. Now there's a pie in your hair."

She was fired before she could take off her apron.

That night she put me in the car, and the two of us drove four hours to Skelly's house in Pennsylvania.

That's my grandfather's nickname, by the way. Skelly. His real name is Sherman Kelly Moon. But when he was a kid, he hated the Sherman part. So he started signing his name "S. Kelly Moon." And he ended up as Skelly.

Anyhow, Ma still hadn't thought of a name for me when we moved into Skelly's. That is, unless you consider "the Little Screamer from Hell" a proper name. But from the first second he saw me, my grandfather started calling me Jake. So that's what I was christened. And the three of us have lived together in his house ever since.

Skelly helped raise me while my mother went back to school. He doesn't remember any of this now. Not even my name. But I'll always be grateful to him for calling me something normal. It's important to have a name you like, I think. Especially when you're a kid. Life is tough enough for a kid without having to stand up at your desk on the first day of school and announce that your name is Yehudi or Prunella or something.

6

There was a kid in my first-grade class named Thorbert Piddler. Even in first grade, we knew this kid's parents had really dumped on him with that one. He looked exactly like you would expect a Thorbert Piddler to look, too. Skinny, with thin, mousy brown hair and huge glasses.

It's a theory of mine that most people grow up to look like their name. Like, in my opinion, if your name is Brunhilda, you can pretty much forget about ever becoming Miss America. Miss America is for people named Tara and Heather and Shawntel. If your name is Brunhilda, you're probably going to drive a cement truck.

In the case of Thorbert Piddler, the best he could have hoped for was to be good at chess, I think. But, because of my grandfather, Thorbert lucked out. In first grade, Skelly volunteered to be our room mother. Which I thought might be weird. But Skelly could bake the most delicious chocolate cupcakes you ever put in your mouth, and when he brought them to school, he'd let me pass them out. So on cupcake days, I was always the most popular kid in the room.

As for Thorbert Piddler, Skelly simply refused to call him Thorbert.

Instead, whenever he came to our class, he'd call out in this great, booming voice, "Where's Thor, God of Thunder?" Then he'd find Thorbert, hoist him onto his shoulders, and carry him around the room.

My grandfather is a big man. Six feet four, almost. So sitting on his shoulders could make you feel like king of the planet. And if you were also imagining yourself to be

"Thor, God of Thunder," well, all I'm saying is that the combination of the two experiences could seriously improve a little kid's self-image.

Like in Thor's case, three or four weeks after Skelly started carrying him around, he stopped crying in class. And by the end of October, his hair started coming in thicker. By mid-November, Thor's voice had gotten loud enough for him to have a speaking role in our class play about the first Thanksgiving. I still remember how straight and tall he stood on the stage as he loudly declared, "I am a cranberry, Squanto!"

Skelly just had that kind of effect on people. He had a way of believing in you, that made you want to believe in yourself.

Like when I was in second grade for instance, my main goal in life was to do three pull-ups in P.E. I wasn't very strong back then. But I was pretty sure three pull-ups would be enough to stop the kids from calling me "noodle arms" when I dangled from the high bar. I swear, though, no matter how hard I pulled and grunted and kicked my legs, I could never lift myself more than an inch or two.

It was frustrating as anything. One day, I strained so hard I wet my pants a little. No one saw. But that night at dinner, I took one look at the noodle casserole on my plate and started to cry.

After a lot of prodding, my mother finally got me to admit the truth. I was a weakling. "A total wuss," I told her. But as Ma reached out to hug me, Skelly stood up from the table, took me by the hand, and led me outside to the backyard tree.

He pointed to a strong, thin branch and lifted me up.

"Grab a hold," he told me.

"No, Skelly, I can't. I can't do this," I whined.

But the second I grabbed the branch, Skelly slipped his hands underneath the bottoms of my shoes. And with something solid to push against, I automatically began to pull.

Skelly urged me on. "Atta boy, Jake. Atta boy."

Slowly my chin rose higher and higher, until it finally touched the branch.

My grandfather let out a whoop. Then he grabbed me and swung me all around in the air. And I mean, even while I was twirling, I knew that I hadn't really done it on my own or anything. But sometimes a shallow little victory is all the victory you need to keep going. Because the next night, I wanted to go out there again. And the night after that, too. And then pretty soon, working on pull-ups after dinner became a routine with Skelly and me.

It was just getting dark the night in April when I went up for my third pull-up and *made* it.

While I was still hanging in mid-air, Skelly hugged me so tight, a little whoosh of air came out of my mouth.

"You're really somethin', Jake Moon," he said in my ear. And I thought I would bust open with pride.

It must have been the same way Thor Piddler felt when he belted out that he was a cranberry that Thanksgiving in first grade. You don't forget amazing moments in your life like that. And you don't forget the people who helped cheer you on, either. Which is why I wasn't surprised at all when, in third grade, Thor showed up at our front door to say good-bye to my grandfather. His dad had been transferred out of state, and while Thor was packing for the move, he ran across an old picture of himself sitting on Skelly's shoulders. And he wanted Skelly to have it to remember him by.

It was a rainy Saturday in November when he came by. The reason I know it was November is because it was the same month that Skelly was diagnosed with Alzheimer's disease.

You've probably heard of Alzheimer's by now. It's that terrible, incurable brain disease that destroys a person's memory, and his ability to think straight, or even to have a simple conversation.

Back then, though, I mostly just thought that Alzheimer's was a disease that made old people forget where they put their car keys. And since I was already used to Skelly being a little absentminded, no big deal, I thought.

Wrong. *Very* big deal. After he was diagnosed, Skelly's normally calm personality turned totally inside out. Ma said it was because he was scared to death about what was happening to him. Now, if he lost his car keys, he would storm around the house looking under everything in sight trying to find them. Even things that made no sense, I mean. Like the microwave oven. Or Ma's ficus plant in the dining room. If he still couldn't find them, he would blame it on me.

"What'd you do with them, Jake? Where'd you put them? From now on you leave my stuff alone! You hear?"

"I didn't take them, Skelly!" I'd yell back. "I didn't touch your stupid keys!"

But nothing I said ever undid his anger. And I'd almost always end up in tears.

Anyhow, it definitely didn't help matters for Skelly to open the front door that rainy Saturday morning and see Thorbert Piddler standing on the porch. Because I'm telling you right now, he didn't have a clue who the kid was.

Not even when Thorbert said he was Thorbert.

My mother and I were both standing there when it happened. And I admit we overreacted a little. Ma yanked Thor into the house by his arm. And I started saying his name over and over again, real loud, like if I said it long enough, or loud enough, it might jog Skelly's memory.

"Thorbert! It's Thor! Look! Thorbert Piddler! It's Thorbert!"

When it still didn't register in Skelly's face, Ma tried as nice as she could to help him along.

"Thor, Dad," she said. "You remember Thor, don't you? From first grade? You were room mother back then, remember? This is Thor, God of Thunder."

Without any warning, Skelly started to yell. "Lord, you two! You don't need to keep saying his name! I'm not crazy yet, am I? I remember Thor! How could I not remember Thor?"

My face heated up in embarrassment.

I laughed, stupidly.

Poor Thor. All he wanted to do was get the heck out of

11

there. He shoved the picture into Skelly's hands and started backing toward the door.

"Yeah, well, I just came to bring you this, Mr. Moon," he said. "I just wanted you to have that picture there, okay? I found it in my closet, and I thought maybe you'd like to have it. But if you don't, you know . . . that's okay, too."

As soon as my grandfather looked at the picture, his face softened.

It was in a silver picture frame with a blue velvet ribbon tied around it. You could tell that Thor had tied the bow himself.

Skelly bent down and put his hand on Thor's shoulder.

"We had fun back then, didn't we, son?" he said.

He smiled a little.

Then he stood back up and turned away.

Early the next morning, when it was still dark outside, I woke up to go to the bathroom. On my way back, I heard a noise coming from the living room.

I tiptoed down the hall and peeked my head around the corner. Skelly was sitting across the room in his favorite rocking chair, rocking in the dark.

As I watched, he stopped rocking and clicked on his flashlight. He shined the light at something he was holding on his lap, looked at it a minute, then clicked off the light and started rocking again.

He did this four or five times before I finally figured out what was going on. Skelly was shining the flashlight on the picture of Thor. Trying to remember.

I went in.

Embarrassed, Skelly quickly pushed everything from his lap to the floor. "What're you doing up?" he said.

Instead of answering, I walked over to the couch and grabbed the afghan that was hanging across the back. Then I climbed into his lap and covered us both with the blanket.

I buried my face in his chest.

"It's cold in here," I said quietly.

Skelly circled his arms around me and held me close as we rocked back and forth.

3
Be-hinds and Other Family Matters

That February, I was chosen class Valentine King. In Mr. Gooding's third grade, the Valentine King was the first boy in the room to hand in the Valentine's Day math assignment with no mistakes. The winner got to wear a king's crown at the party and join the Valentine Queen in passing out all the cards from the valentine box.

The Valentine Queen was Lila Lilly. Lila was a quiet girl with braces, so I had no reason to expect trouble out of her. But as soon as Mr. Gooding gave her that stupid crown, it must have gone to her head or something, because she knocked me out of the way, dug both arms into the box, and took about 90 percent of the valentines for herself. Then, somehow, she held out her skirt as a pouch for the cards, and she started dashing around the room like she was Delivery Queen of the World.

Annoyed, I took off after her to discuss the matter. And okay, fine, I admit there was a scuffle. But still, I don't think it was a big enough deal to make me forfeit my crown, *plus* not get a valentine cupcake.

Anyhow, since Mr. Gooding was the kind of teacher who enjoyed calling parents at home at night, I thought it would be smart to tell Ma my side of the story before he squealed. And in another smart move, I decided to save my confession for the dinner table, where Ma was less likely to take a swat at me. But I had barely gotten to the part about Lila Lilly being Valentine Queen when Skelly interrupted.

"We used to have an old dog named Queenie. Remember Queenie, Mavis?" he said. "She had pups in my sleeping bag one time."

I frowned at him. "Yeah, great, Skell. But I really need to tell Ma about what happened at school today, okay?"

My grandfather paid no attention to me at all. "Wait, hold it. I'm wrong. I'm thinking of Heidi."

"Yeah, well, whatever," I said, turning back to my mother. "So, anyway, when Lila—"

"Remember Heidi, Mavis?" said Skelly. "She had one brown ear and one white ear. Got her from the pound. Only had three legs. Remember her?"

I could tell by Ma's face that something wasn't right here, but she didn't correct him.

Suddenly, Skelly shook his head. "No. Hold on again. That was my old friend Hiram Wickham, wasn't it?"

I raised my eyebrows. What was this? Hiram Wickham had three legs?

I started to ask what he was talking about, but Ma kicked me under the table.

"Poor old Hiram," said Skelly. "Had to have two of his dogs amputated. Ran over them with his lawn mower.

Remember that, Mavis? The big dog and the little one."

Now I was stunned. Hiram had amputated his *dogs*?

Quickly, Ma leaned in my direction and shook her head. *"Toes,"* she whispered so my grandfather couldn't hear. "Hiram Wickham ran over two of his toes. Not his dogs."

That night, after my mother and Skelly left the table, I sat there contemplating the horrors of Hiram Wickham, and how completely mixed up Skelly had gotten.

After she finished the dishes, Ma came over and tried to turn up the corners of my mouth with her fingers. I pushed her hand away.

"He's getting worse, Ma," I said. "Tonight when he messed up, he didn't even know it. He didn't even catch himself."

My mother smoothed my hair. Her silence told me I was right.

After she left, I went to the living room.

For the rest of the night, I sat across from Skelly's recliner and watched him watch TV.

I hardly blinked.

Hardly even moved.

Maybe if I watched him close enough, he wouldn't have a chance to slip further away.

Alzheimer's has three stages. Each stage is worse than the one before it. I don't know if any of the stages have official names, but in my head, I think of them as (1) sad, (2) sadder, and (3) the saddest thing you've ever seen.

Skelly's doc is a woman named Dr. Bloomfield. She told Ma and me that there's no set time period for how long each stage lasts. And that since not all patients have the same symptoms, you're never sure exactly when a person has passed from one terrible stage to the next terrible stage.

The day I started fourth grade, I went to get a can of orange juice and found Skelly's pajamas in the freezer. It might sound funny. But it was the second time he'd put them in there instead of the hamper, so I didn't get a big hearty laugh out of it or anything.

A few days later, when I brought my new best friend, Lucas Carney, home from school, there was a little note on the freezer in Skelly's handwriting. It said, THIS IS NOT THE HAMPER.

Lucas looked at it. Then at me.

I tried to laugh it off. "Oh *that*. That's just some stupid joke between Ma and me," I said. To distract him, I poured us something to drink.

But just as I was handing Lucas his glass, we both noticed a piece of material sticking out the top of the oven door.

Lucas pulled it open.

Inside, on the top rack, were two wet sheets.

"Is this another joke between your mother and you, or do you guys dry your sheets in the oven?" he asked.

This time, I started to stammer like you wouldn't believe. "Yeah, we do. I mean, no, we don't. I mean, the thing is, our dryer broke this morning before I left for school. And Ma read in our oven book that if you're really in a bind, you can dry wet clothes in the oven."

Lucas put his hand inside the door. "But it isn't even on."

My mind was racing a mile a minute. "I know, I know. I mean, of course it's not on. If you turn on the heat, the sheets will burn to a crisp. The book said that sheets are supposed to dry in their own natural juices."

I closed the oven door and pointed Lucas toward my room. "Go pick out a video game, okay? I'll be there in a minute."

As soon as he was gone, I looked through the kitchen window and saw Skelly working in the yard. He was hunched over in the middle of the grass. Pulling out weeds, it looked like.

I hurried to the back door and locked it.

Then I ran straight to my room and I locked that door, too.

Skelly was still outside when Ma got home from work that afternoon.

Lucas had gone by then. So as soon as I heard her car pull up, I ran out and tattled on my grandfather like he was a little kid. "You've gotta talk to him, Ma. You've got to. He embarrassed me so bad today. He's not even *trying*. He's just being an idiot."

After she heard all the details, my mother said she'd find a way to mention the sheets to him. But at dinner that night, Skelly was in such good spirits, she didn't want to ruin his mood.

Halfway through supper, he looked at me and snapped his fingers. "Oops . . . almost forgot, Jakie boy," he said. "Look what I found while I was digging out in the garden today."

He reached into his shirt pocket and pulled out one of my old Matchbox race cars.

He rolled it to me across the table. "This was always one of your favorites, wasn't it?" he said.

I turned it over in my hand. It was the red Ferrari with the blazes of fire painted on the sides. He must have been polishing it up all afternoon. He'd even touched up the paint and gotten the rust and dirt out of the little tire rims.

I thanked him and reached over to give him a hug. But as I did, my mind flashed an ugly instant replay of how I'd locked the back door so he couldn't get in.

I kicked myself around pretty good over that, too. But that's how up and down and unpredictable our lives were back then. Just when you were sure Skelly had gone off the deep end for good, he'd start acting like his regular old self, almost.

Later, I asked Ma not to mention the sheets thing to him. But she told me she already had. And in a little bit of a breakthrough, she said Skelly had seemed willing to post more notes around the house to help him remember things better.

The next morning when I got up, little Post-it notes were taped all over the place. Like, on the phone receivers were notes shouting, TAKE MESSAGE!!! And there were larger notes on the appliances. Like a CLOSE ME sign on the refrigerator door. And a TURN ME OFF sign on the stove top.

Also, Ma had made Skelly a list of reminders, which she pinned to the bottom of his shirt. Things like: (1) turn off hose, (2) turn off stove burners, (3) lock front door, and (4) wash goes in dryer.

She pinned the list upside down, so all he had to do was hold it out and read it. But as helpful as it was to him, it made me sad as anything seeing that list pinned to him all the time. He looked like some forgetful little kindergartner with a note from his teacher.

Since my mother is an accountant, she was able to adjust her schedule to work at home during the morning and not leave for the office till noon. She was home again at four thirty. Meanwhile, an older lady from across the street, named Etta Gerber, looked in on Skelly once or twice till I got home from school at three thirty.

Etta came over again at four, just to "double-check on the Moon men," she used to say. She thought that was a hilarious joke, by the way. She acted like she was the first person who had ever thought of it.

Usually when I got home from school, Skelly was either working in the yard or down in his basement workshop. All of his life my grandfather had been a house painter. But after he retired, he started restoring old furniture and antiques. He was a real craftsman, too. Skelly could take some scummy old table that you wouldn't even want to touch, and in a month or two he could have it looking like new.

He always let me help him, too. Even when I was little and sloppy, if I asked to help, Skelly would stop what he was doing and teach me how to do the job right. He never made up some pretend little job for me just so I'd stay out of his hair, like some dads do. And he wasn't afraid to let me mess up, either. "Sometimes, messin' up is the best teacher," he used to say.

A couple of weeks ago, I was walking past this house down the street, and there was this little girl who thought she was helping her dad paint the porch steps. But even though her hand was on the brush, her dad's hand was right on top of hers, doing the actual painting so she wouldn't slop it up. And I'm sure the guy meant well and all. But how's the kid ever supposed to learn, you know?

When Skelly taught me how to paint, he showed me exactly how far to dip the brush in the can. And how to tap it lightly on the edge to shake off the extra so it didn't drip and run. It paid off, too. I was the only kid in my kindergarten class who didn't splat paint all over the room on the first day of art. Not one drop anywhere, I mean. I got my first happy face sticker for that.

When I think about it, Skelly taught me a ton of stuff in that basement workshop of his. Sometimes, he taught me stuff he wasn't even aware of, I don't think. Like the first time I helped him sand a table, the two of us didn't talk for over thirty minutes, I bet. Just stood there working side by side, listening to the rhythm of the sand paper as it rubbed back and forth across the wood. Even now, I still love the sound of that.

We were excellent sanders, Skelly and me. We could sand a piece of wood till it was as smooth as a baby's behind.

That was one of his favorite expressions, by the way. Smooth as a baby's behind. Except he pronounced it *"be*-hind," with the accent on the *be*. Which always made me laugh, because it sounded particularly stupid that way.

The last project my grandfather ever worked on down there was a scuzzy little table my aunt Marguerite bought at a yard sale. Aunt Marguerite is one of those yard sale crazies that you hear about sometimes. Like if you're having a yard sale that starts at seven, she's the one pounding on your screen door at five in the morning asking why the stuff isn't in the carport yet.

She gets first dibs on the bargains that way, she says. That totally kills me, too, because in her divorce settlement Aunt Marguerite got so much money you can't count the zeros.

Anyhow, as soon as she bought it, she brought the scuzzy table straight over to Skelly to refinish for her. And to make things even more unpleasant, she also brought my scuzzy cousin James, who's a year older than me. And who I've never liked. And who treats me like I'm gum on the bottom of his shoe.

By the time Skelly and I walked out to see the table, James had already unloaded it onto the sidewalk. But even though it was out in the open air, I still had to hold my nose when I got close to it. I'm not kidding. The stink pollution coming from that little table was contaminating the entire neighborhood.

I could not believe my ears when Aunt Marguerite told James to pick it up and take it to Skelly's workshop.

I let go of my nose. "No! Geez! Doesn't anybody notice that pukey smell but me? Come on, Aunt Marguerite. At least let it air out for a while. There are people who have to *live* in that house."

By this time, James had managed to get the table to the bottom of the porch steps.

I ran over and grabbed the other side of it.

"Put it down, James. We're not taking it in yet," I said.

James tried to pull it away. "Knock it off, *Joke*."

"No, you knock it off, *Lames*," I said back. Then, still holding on to the table, I gave a hard push and shoved him backward.

James tripped over his feet and the table fell on its side. That's when my grandfather came rushing over. There was nothing that annoyed Skelly more than when me and James fought. Which was always.

"Lord save us, you two. Give it here! I'll carry it to the basement myself!" he snapped.

Angrily, he picked it up and hurried up the stoop.

Aunt Marguerite gave me and James one of her classic looks and told Skelly to be careful.

I followed them into the house.

When they got to the end of the hall, my grandfather waited while my aunt opened the basement door and flipped on the light switch.

I watched as Skelly hoisted the table higher in his arms and headed down. But instead of taking each step slowly, in his anger he was still going much too fast.

Aunt Marguerite shouted for him to slow down.

I closed my eyes.

He was four steps from the bottom when he fell.

4

Lucky Duck

He broke his wrists.

Both of them.

But still, there wasn't one person in the emergency room that night who didn't go on and on about Skelly's wonderful good luck.

"You're a lucky man, Mr. Moon," said the emergency room doctor. "You could have broken your neck in a fall like that."

"His neck?" said the nurse. "He's lucky he didn't break his back."

The X-ray guy was my favorite. He held the pictures of Skelly's two shattered wrist bones up to the light and said, "Considering how far you fell, I'd say you've got yourself a couple of lucky breaks here."

He cracked up at his own stupid joke. When he looked at me to see if I was laughing, too, I wasn't.

I mean, excuse me, okay? But for an old man whose biggest joy in life is sanding old furniture, it seems like two broken wrists are a pretty huge deal. And if the doctor, or the nurse, or the X-ray guy, hadn't been so busy yucking it up, maybe they would have noticed that my grandfather hadn't spoken two words to any of them.

As we rode home in the car, I sat next to Skelly in the backseat. Every time I looked over at him, he was staring at his casts. He never took his eyes off of them once. And even days later, long after he should have been used to them, I would walk into the living room and find him sitting in his recliner watching his casts, instead of the TV.

"Hey, Skell. What's up?" I would say. "Isn't there something you want to watch on the tube?" Then right away, I'd start flipping through the channels trying to find a basketball game or something else he might like.

But no matter what I picked for him, it wasn't long before his eyes would drop. And he'd be right back staring at those casts again.

Dr. Bloomfield wasn't surprised by his gloominess. She said it was common for Alzheimer's patients to get depressed after going through a trauma like his. She even warned us that the disease might start getting worse faster.

"After a trauma, patients can become so overwhelmed it's almost like they don't have the energy to keep fighting anymore," she told us.

To try and lift his spirits, my mother and my aunt took him on picnics on the weekends. Other times, me and Ma would take him to the movies, or out for ice cream.

But regardless of what we did, the minute Skelly hit the door, he'd head straight for his recliner or his bed.

To their credit, Ma and Marguerite didn't give up. In fact, the week before his casts finally came off, my aunt brought him a small burlap sack with a big red ribbon tied around it. Inside were packages of flower seeds. All of Skelly's favorites.

She hurried into his room and woke him.

"Look, Dad. Flower seeds! See them? Pansies, poppies, morning glories! I know it's still too cool to plant them outside, but I bought everything you need to get them started inside. Fluorescent bulbs, potting soil . . . it's all in the kitchen. You can grow them from seed and then transplant them in your garden as soon as it warms up."

She showed him the pictures of the flowers. "Just a few more weeks and you'll be out there with your trowel, digging in the garden just like always."

Skelly's eyes filled with tears. We thought it was because he was so happy that his troubles were almost over. But the next day when I got up, I found the bag of flower seeds in the kitchen trash, where he'd dumped them during the night.

Ma tried to shrug it off. "It was just too soon for him to think about all that," she said. "You mark my words, Jake. As soon as those casts come off, he'll be rarin' to get started."

But one week later, when the casts did come off, Skelly was more worried about his wrists than ever. At dinner the first night, he wouldn't even carry a plate of spaghetti to the table. He said it was too heavy. And at breakfast the next morning, he had both wrists wrapped in brown socks. Which was just plain disturbing.

That afternoon, I dug out his old baseball glove from his closet and told him I'd like to have a catch. It just seemed like a good way to ease him back into using his hands again, I thought.

"Come on, Skell. It'll be fun," I said. "We'll take it totally easy. I promise."

At first, Skelly examined the glove like he was trying to figure out what it was. But when he finally looked up at me from his chair, his expression had turned sour.

"*Catch*? Exactly how am I supposed to play catch?" He said the word like it was a bad taste in his mouth. Then he threw the glove on the floor and stood up.

The next thing I knew, he was flinging his wrists in my face. "How am I supposed to do anything at all with bones as weak as these? Huh? Tell me that, will you? How am I going to do anything ever again?"

As he turned and left the room, I heard him mutter, "*Catch,* for Christ's sake."

Skelly had never sworn around me before. Never once in my whole life.

With tears running down my face, I picked up his glove and took it outside. Then I lifted the lid off the trash can and slammed it straight to the bottom.

Four months after his accident, I woke Skelly up for dinner one night and he asked me who I was. He said it like a joke, almost. He'd been asleep on his bed, and when I tapped him awake, he said, "Who you?"

"Yeah, right. Real funny, Skell. Ma says the pot roast is ready, okay? Can you smell it?"

He squinted his eyes and studied my face.

That's when I knew that he wasn't joking. He didn't have a clue who I was.

There's no way to describe how terrible that made me feel inside, except to say that it's never totally gone away. And even though there were still times after that when Skelly knew me perfectly well, it became more and more common for me to walk into the room and have him totally baffled.

Over time, Skelly finally settled on the idea that I was Claude Harper. His best friend from when he was a kid.

And now, through the magic of Alzheimer's . . .

His best friend once again.

After my grandfather's accident, Ma took a leave of absence from work to stay with him for a few weeks. Then my aunt Marguerite stayed with him some, too. But eventually both of them had to go back to work, and they hired a full-time caregiver.

A caregiver is a person who takes care of sick people. The caregiver doesn't have to be a nurse, but ours was. Ours was a registered nurse named Lanna. The reason I know she was *registered,* is that it was physically impossible for Lanna to say "I am a nurse" without adding the *registered* part. Like anyone even knows what that means.

My mother's work schedule had changed again. She'd gotten a promotion and was needed at the office in the morning. So for a long time, Lanna came at nine and stayed till Ma got home at four thirty. But by the middle of my fifth grade year, Lanna started having "problems" with her daughter, Vanna. And from then on she needed to leave our house at "three thirty sharp," she said, to pick up Vanna from school.

Ma tried to hire someone to watch Skelly from three thirty to four thirty, but no one was interested. So finally, I offered to fill in for a while.

It didn't seem like it would be a big deal, really. Most of the time I just came home from school and watched TV anyway. And Skelly was almost always asleep in his recliner. So how much of a pain could it be? I thought.

At first, the answer was none at all. In fact, for the first month or so it seemed like nothing had even changed. But pretty soon, stuff started coming up after school that I had to miss. And I began to resent it.

It didn't help that Skelly's behavior kept getting weirder and weirder, either. For one thing, he began roaming around in the middle of the night. Ma installed dead bolts and bells on all the outside doors to keep him from wandering away. But none of that stopped him from shuffling from room to room at three in the morning, turning on all the lights.

Also, he began hoarding stuff from the kitchen. There were nights when I would hear him knocking around in the dark, and when I got up, I'd find him carrying cans of soup and vegetables down the hall to his room. He'd line them up all nice and neat on his shelf, just like the cans in the grocery store.

When I asked him why, he said he needed to have food in there "just in *case*." Whatever that meant.

Another thing that got worse was Skelly's repeating. One Sunday at Family Night dinner, he set a new world record by asking James and me if we liked lima beans eleven times. On the twelfth time, James passed me an imaginary gun under the table, and we pretended to shoot ourselves. So far, it's been one of our nicest moments.

Anyhow, even with all the confusion at home, I was still managing to have a life at school. Lucas Carney was still my best friend in fifth grade, so by then I had told him about Skelly's Alzheimer's. Not all the crazy business, I don't mean. But Lucas definitely knew my grandfather wasn't "all there."

A couple times a week, usually, Lucas would come over after school and we'd shoot hoops in my side yard. We almost always stayed outside while Skelly napped in the living room. But once in a while, we'd go into the kitchen for a drink of water. And on one of those trips, Skelly woke up and came wandering in to join us.

His hair was all wild and fuzzy-looking from the recliner. And he was only wearing one shoe.

As soon as he saw Lucas, he pointed his finger and told him to "zipper his brisket."

I froze in embarrassment. Meanwhile, Lucas started backing up like a pyscho had just entered the room.

Finally, I managed to grab Lucas by the arm and steer him out the door.

"Jacket," I said as soon as we got outside. "He meant to zip your jacket. It's just that the Alzheimer's keeps erasing words from his vocabulary, and when he can't remember the right name for something, he substitutes something else."

Lucas rolled his eyes. "Then why didn't he just tell me to zipper my *coat*? I mean, God, Moon . . . a brisket is like a big hunk of meat or something."

I started getting defensive. "So what do you want me to do, Lucas? Do you want me to figure out a way for this stupid disease to make sense to you? That's just the way it works, okay?"

After that came this awkward kind of silence. Lucas grabbed the ball and started shooting again.

"So?" I said finally.

"So what?"

"So are you going to zipper your brisket or not?"

Lucas laughed a little and zipped up. "There. *Now* is everyone happy?"

Things got back to normal after that. But a couple of weeks later, when Lucas went inside to get another drink, Skelly called him Sylvia.

From that day on, whenever he got thirsty, Lucas Carney drank from our outside hose.

My resentment started to build. I know it was only an hour a day that I had to stay with Skelly. But there turned out to be a big difference between coming home right after school because I *wanted* to, and coming home right after school because I *had* to.

The trouble was, Ma was all the time praising me like I was a saint or something, telling me how generous I was, giving Skelly an hour of my day. Plus she was always saying how she would do everything in her power to keep the rest of my life "as normal as possible."

"Cross my heart and hope to die, Jake," she told me one Saturday morning, "I'm going to hang on to normal if it kills me." Then, to show me she really meant business, she went down to sign me up for Little League an hour before the doors opened.

There were two baseball games a week that spring, plus three practices. But Ma insisted that getting me there would be no problem. It's just that Skelly would have to come with us now. "Who knows?" she said. "Maybe getting him outside in the fresh air with all those young ball players might even do him some good."

Skelly had always loved baseball. He had played on a senior league till he was sixty, I think it was. And we still have the videotape of the time he took me to my first Little League game.

It was the same day I took my first steps, actually. Ma said he was so proud of those five steps, he ran me straight down to the ball field, where there was a game going on.

My mother, who's always had a tendency to overtape my life, ran behind him with the video camera. As soon as the

Little League game was over, she filmed Skelly carrying me around the backstop and standing me up on home plate.

I fell down twice. But the third time, I stood there all by myself for at least ten seconds before I started to sway. Then, just as I was about to keel over, Skelly came running into the picture, scooped me up in his arms, and zoomed me around the bases for my first home run.

Unfortunately, when I played in fifth grade, Ma's wishful thinking about the fresh air being good for Skelly didn't prove to be true. In fact, most of the time, as soon as she got him seated on the bleachers at a game, he was ready to go home again.

Ma kept on bringing him, though. Whenever he got antsy, she would walk him around the track or the school parking lot. I know it was hard on her. And I know she tried her best. But twice during the season, she got busy talking to someone in the stands and Skelly climbed down and started to walk home by himself.

Both times he took a shortcut through the infield.

In the middle of an inning.

The guys on my team started calling him Mr. Magoo, after that old-man cartoon character with the bad eyesight, who's always walking where he shouldn't.

I laughed.

You learn to do that by fifth grade.

If you don't laugh, they never stop.

The last inning of the last game of the season, for some completely unknown reason, my grandfather stood up in his seat and started shouting, "Cold beer! Right here!"

My team was at bat when it happened. I walked out of the dugout and straight to the car. Never said squat to my coach or my teammates or anybody. Just walked to the car and waited for Ma to bring Skelly and drive me home.

Thank God, school got out a week later and I could lay low for a couple of months.

5

Just Say No

By the time sixth grade rolled around in September, the laying low strategy had turned into total boredom, and I was desperate to get out of the house again.

Sixth grade started out pretty good for me, too. Like the second week of school, my teacher asked me if I'd run for class treasurer. And a day or two after that, we got this new kid in our class named Aaron Friar, who was assigned to the seat right next to me. Which was so lucky I couldn't believe. Because you could tell by the way Aaron looked, and dressed—and walked, even—that he was going to be seriously popular.

As soon as he sat down, a plan was already forming in my head. I would hook up with Aaron Friar while he was still desperate for friends, and then shoot straight up the popularity ladder with him.

The second week he was in school, I got the nerve to invite him to spend the night at my house. It had been more than a year since anyone had slept over. With all the problems going on with my grandfather, I'd hardly even thought about stuff like that, in fact.

But even though it was risky having someone in my house with Skelly acting so weird, the opportunity with Aaron was too good to pass up. And besides, if Aaron and I mostly stayed in my room, and Skelly mostly slept in his chair, there was a decent chance that the two of them wouldn't even have to meet.

I planned out the night like you wouldn't believe. First, in a covert operation at school, I got a hold of the latest teenage slasher movie, which Ma had refused to let me rent. Then I drilled it into her head that she was not— under any circumstances—allowed to open my door without knocking first. And even *then* she had to wait for me to say "Come in." That way I'd have more than enough time to click off the VCR. So no problem.

I also told her that she was not allowed to let Skelly out of her sight. Which she already knew, she said. But just to be sure, I kept on mentioning it right up until Aaron's parents dropped him off at my house on Friday.

As soon as he knocked on the door that night, I whisked him straight to my room. Then I shut the door and opened a brand-new video game I had bought with my allowance. An hour or so later, my mother kept her word and kicked the door about ten times with her foot before carrying in a big bucket of chicken for us to eat in the room.

Aaron was having a good time, too. You could tell he was. And the movie was only going to make it better.

Or at least that's what I thought.

But as the two of us were finishing our chicken, there was another noise at my door. It was Ma bringing dessert, I figured, so I didn't pay much attention.

But when the door pushed open, it wasn't my mother at all.

It was . . . guess who.

Skelly had been on his way to the shower and had heard our voices. So he wandered on in and stood in the middle of my room.

And he wasn't wearing pants.

No pants at all, I mean.

No long pants.

No short pants.

No underpants.

And Aaron Friar busted out laughing so hard that orange soda came out his nose.

He didn't stop, either. Not even when Ma ran in apologizing all over the place, and rushed Skelly back out the door. Not even when I explained to him about the Alzheimer's. Or swore that Skelly had never done anything like this ever before.

I begged him not to say anything.

"Come on, Aaron. Please don't tell anybody at school, okay? I mean, what if this was your grandfather? What if *he* had an incurable brain disease? You wouldn't want people cracking jokes about him, would you?"

I never should have used the word *crack*. Aaron busted out all over again.

Now I was getting mad.

"Okay. Knock it off, Aaron. I mean it. How can you laugh at someone who's sick like that? It's only going to get worse, too. He's going to die from it, okay? How can that be funny to you?"

Aaron stopped laughing then. He was sorry, he said. He hadn't known Skelly was going to die. He *got it* now, he told me. And he swore he would never mention what happened to anyone. He *swore*.

On Monday morning, I walked past a group of guys on the playground. A kid I hardly knew cupped his hands around his mouth and shouted, "Hey, Moon! I hear your grandpa's a perv!"

It's been two and a half years since Aaron Friar spent the night.

No kid's been invited to my house since.

I dropped out of the race for class treasurer. My mother begged me not to. But I knew it would be asking for trouble. Dirty campaigns are a fact of life, and there are too many words that rhyme with *perv*.

Later that month, I decided not to go out for cross-country. And in October I stayed home from basketball tryouts. By then, Ma was going nuts practically, swearing up and down again that we could still make it all work. But I'm not one of those kids who can brush off humiliation like it's a crumb on my shirt. And the idea that Skelly would be sitting in the stands in my school gym during a basketball game made me crazy, almost.

No gets easier the more you say it. And as the year went on, I got better and better at making up excuses and turning down invitations. The logic was as simple as my new life. If I didn't go to anyone's house, no one would expect to come to mine.

It takes a while for friends to stop calling, but eventually they do. The house stays a lot quieter when the phone doesn't ring. Which is depressing at first. But if no one calls, at least your grandfather can't pick up the phone while he's watching *Wheel of Fortune* and tell Lucas Carney that he'd like to buy a vowel.

The night that happened, Lucas laughed about it. But I could tell from his voice that it had creeped him out again. And before he hung up, he asked if from now on I could answer the phone before Skelly did.

It bothered me that he would ask that, but I said I'd try. But trying must not have been good enough, because Lucas didn't call me anymore after that. And so what had started out as a perfectly good school year had turned totally rotten by Christmas.

Just to show you how weird life can be, though, on the first day back from winter break, something came up that almost turned everything around. It was almost time for the afternoon bell to ring, when my teacher started handing out permission slips for music lessons. As usual, I began passing the whole stack to the kid behind me without bothering to take one.

And then, out of nowhere, it hit me!

Music lessons.

The *drums!*

I could take *drum* lessons!

It was perfect. Everything about drum lessons would fit right into my life. Since I was still watching Skelly after school, I had tons of time to practice. Plus, I'd be learning a valuable skill. Plus, Ma wouldn't have to drag Skelly out in public to watch me. Plus, playing the drums was just plain cool.

As soon as I got home that day, I called Ma at the office. I was breathless almost, trying to get it all out.

"The lessons are on Monday and Thursday afternoons. But they're only for an hour, Ma. So I was thinking that maybe Lanna could stay extra for those two days. *Please,* Ma. Just figure out a way for me to take these lessons and I'll never ask you for another thing. I swear. I promise. I swear."

The next morning, my mother offered to pay Lanna twice her normal hourly salary for those two extra hours a week if she would please stay. She even offered to send a cab for Vanna on the days of my drum lessons, and bring her over to the house.

When Lanna said no, Ma offered the job to Etta Gerber across the street.

When Etta Gerber said she was working full-time in a tropical-fish store, Ma put an ad in the paper for a new nurse.

By the first drum lesson, six people had called for interviews. By the second drum lesson, Ma had interviewed two of them. Both cranky.

By the third drum lesson, she'd interviewed the other four. All too expensive.

By the fourth drum lesson, I'd already missed four drum lessons, and the music teacher said it was too late to catch up.

My mother promised I could take drum lessons in the summer.

By the summer, I didn't care.

It took over a year for me to completely accept it. But as hard as she had tried, my mother had not been able to "hang on to normal."

Even before the start of seventh grade, I had officially stopped thinking of myself as a regular kid and had begun thinking of myself as a kid with obligations at home.

The first week of P.E., when Coach Rob passed out slips to play on our seventh-grade flag football league, I wadded mine up and shot it into the trash can on my way out of the gym.

I never gave it another thought after that. I promise I didn't.

But then on the day of the first practice game, I was walking across the playground on my way home from school and this friend of mine on the team—a kid named Harris Reilly—was tossing around a football. And he yelled at me to go out for a pass.

And so just for the heck of it, I did.

I caught the ball and threw it back.

Harris backed up. "Go long!" he shouted.

I turned around and started to run downfield. The ball sailed in the air, up and out, and over my head. I ran faster and faster, as fast as I could go.

At the very last minute, I reached my arms and stretched my fingers to their limit.

The next thing I knew, I was traveling sideways through the air. Flying, almost.

Then, *smack*! Just as I caught the ball, I hit the ground, belly first, and started rolling around and laughing so hard I couldn't stop.

I mean, it just felt so *good,* you know? Running and laughing and diving into the grass like that. And more than anything, I wanted to stay and watch the game.

I looked at my watch. I was already late. Lanna would be mad.

I took off running for home. In fact, I was almost out the school gate when this totally unexpected thought came breezing through my brain.

So what?

I stopped cold.

No, *really. So what* if Lanna was mad? Was the world going to come to an end? Would the earth explode if Lanna didn't pick Vanna up at exactly two forty-five?

I'm telling you, the idea was so freeing, I can't even describe it.

I turned around, walked back to the sidelines, and sat down.

Twenty minutes later, I was still sitting there when Ma's car pulled into the parking lot.

When she got out, she started walking that heavy-footed kind of walk that mothers do when they're so out of control they don't care who knows it.

Skelly was a few feet behind her. I'm sure she had told him to stay in the car, but he'd already forgotten. Even from the football field, I could see that he had dressed himself again. He was wearing pajama bottoms with suspenders, plus a wool scarf.

I jumped up and started running toward them. I prayed as I ran. Please, Ma. Oh God, please. Just don't start shouting. Not in front of all these kids.

I was almost there when the explosion came.

"WHERE IN GOD'S NAME HAVE YOU BEEN!?!"

Her voice was loud and screechy, and it carried in the wind.

I could feel the eyes of the entire football team staring at my back. Panicking, I brought my finger to my lips and made the *shh* sound.

Big mistake.

My mother's voice went up an entire octave. "Oh, no, you don't! Do not try to shush me, mister! Do you have any idea the trouble you've caused? Do you? Do you?"

She lunged for my arm then and started marching me to the car. When she saw Skelly, she grabbed him, too. And the three of us paraded across the grass like jolly members of the "Hey, Look at Us . . . We're Insane!" family.

We drove home in silence.

When we were almost there, Skelly looked over the seat at me and waved his fingers.

I glared at him in his stupid striped pajamas with his idiotic brain disease.

I hated him.

6

The Nut

Lanna quit.

She said Vanna got so upset when she wasn't picked up on time, she tore up her three-ring binder and stomped on her lunch box.

Vanna is a freak.

The timing of Lanna's "I quit" call couldn't have been worse, either. Ma had just cooled down from her tirade at school and was apologizing for going ballistic. It was just "one of those days" she said. She was getting a cold, and it had been a bad day at work, plus Skelly had been particularly stubborn all afternoon.

She was trying to get me to say that I forgave her, which I hadn't yet, when Lanna called. Five minutes into the conversation, Ma laid the receiver down next to the phone and went to her room.

Even with the door shut, I could hear her crying in there. I didn't go in, though. Sometimes when my mother gets real low like that, she needs to talk. Other times, she just needs to be alone.

Lanna gave Ma and Aunt Marguerite two weeks to find another nurse. The next day, they started calling hospitals and nursing homes and any place else that had a medical staff who worked with old people. Eventually, Ma called the senior citizens' center not far from our house, and Alma Russell answered the phone.

It turned out to be one of those weird coincidences that happen in life sometimes. Or, who knows, maybe it was fate. But as soon as my mother introduced herself, Mrs. Russell let out a whoop of surprise, and she said that she and "the lovely Mr. Skelly Moon" had grown up on the very same street together.

Two hours later, Mrs. Russell called back and said she wanted the job.

Just like Lanna, Mrs. Russell was a registered nurse. She had been working at the Senior Center for years and was used to dealing with Alzheimer's patients. Ma and Aunt Marguerite checked out her background and hired her the same day of her interview.

As a special added bonus, Mrs. Russell was single, with no family of her own. So she could help out late at night and on weekends if we needed her.

Looking back, I think that hiring Alma Russell was one of the best things that ever happened to my grandfather. I mean, it's true that she's turned out to have a few quirks we didn't count on. But no one could do a better job of taking care of Skelly than she does. Ma says it's magical, the way Mrs. Russell automatically knows what's bothering Skelly when no one else has a clue.

Still, like I said, she *is* a little quirky, and getting used to her has taken some time. In fact, she's worked for us for almost a year and a half now, and there are still days that I don't think I'm totally there yet.

For one thing, there is no *Mr.* Russell. Which wouldn't be that unusual, except that—as far as anyone knows—there's *never* been a Mr. Russell. All Ma knows for sure is that in 1963 Miss Alma Shlossman flew to Las Vegas for a week. And she came back calling herself Mrs. Alma Russell.

That's all she came back with, too. The new name. No new husband. No new wedding pictures. No new anything else.

We'll probably never get to the bottom of what really happened out there. My mother casually mentioned the city of Las Vegas to her while they were folding laundry once, and Mrs. Russell picked up the basket, went out the back door, and finished folding in the yard.

Also, just for the record, Alma Russell always dresses in a nurse's uniform. *Always,* I mean. Like even on her days off, when she's mowing her lawn or washing her car, she wears a white dress, white shoes, and those white, swishy nurse's stockings. Twice—when we've taken her to a nice restaurant for dinner—she's added a nurse's cap to "dress things up."

My mother calls Mrs. Russell a godsend. But if God sent us Mrs. Russell, I'm pretty sure she was meant to be a gag gift.

Still, for as much as she gets on my nerves, I owe Mrs. Russell a debt so big I will never be able to repay it.

It was Mrs. Russell who came to Skelly's rescue that terrible afternoon when I saw him in the school Dumpster.

It's funny how when you try not to think about something, you think about it all the more. The details are still clear in my mind. Like I still remember the mocking tone in both those kids' voices when they shouted their insults at Skelly. And how, when they finally walked away, my grandfather kept waving until they turned the corner.

Not long after that, one of the school custodians spotted him and went running over to help. He didn't yell at Skelly or anything. Just motioned for him to get out. But my grandfather can be stubborn sometimes, and he didn't budge. I was still trying to force myself to go over and help when the custodian spotted Skelly's Medic Alert ID necklace. He took out his cell phone and called our number.

Since we only live a few houses from the school, Mrs. Russell was there in less than five minutes.

I can't tell you how relieved I felt when I saw her flying around the corner, full speed ahead. It was the same feeling you get when the cavalry charges in to save the day at the end of those old Westerns you see sometimes. I mean it. If there had been a bugle playing in the background as she ran, it wouldn't have seemed out of place to me at all.

Considering how fast she was running, I thought she might try to fling herself up and over the top of the Dumpster. But as soon as Skelly spotted her, she slowed to a walk. Even though I was too far away to hear her voice, I could tell she was talking to him the whole time. And within only a minute or two, he was climbing back out of the Dumpster.

Mrs. Russell hugged him. Then brushed him off. Then hugged him some more.

After that, she put her arm around Skelly's waist and led him home.

That night, Ma made Skelly's favorite dinner—meat loaf and mashed potatoes. In between bites, her eyes would fill up and she'd grab a hold of his hand and tell him how "deeply and sincerely sorry" she was for what had happened.

It turned out to be her fault that Skelly had wandered away from the house. She'd forgotten to lock the front-door dead bolt with her key.

As for Skelly, he didn't even remember he'd been in the Dumpster.

As for me, I could only imagine how proud Ma would have been to know I had seen the whole thing and done nothing to help.

I choked down some meat loaf and left the table as soon as I could.

I went to bed early that night, and tossed and turned for hours it seemed.

By the time I got up the next morning, my mother was already in Skelly's room, getting him ready to take out to breakfast. It was her way of apologizing even more, I think. Skelly has always loved going out to breakfast, and it's one of the few things about him that Alzheimer's hasn't changed. Ma takes him to the House of Pancakes at least once a month.

I used to go with them, but lately, almost never. So when I asked if I could come this time, Ma looked shocked.

"Are you *serious*?" she asked me. "And to what do my dear father and I owe this very great honor?"

I shrugged it off.

What was I supposed to say? "Oh yeah . . . I forgot to tell you. Remember yesterday when the janitor found Skelly in the Dumpster? Well, see, I already knew he was there, Ma. In fact, a couple of guys I know were getting a big kick out of mocking him. So I'm sure you can understand how awkward it would have been to admit he was my grandfather. But then last night, my conscience wouldn't let me sleep that good. So I figured that maybe coming out to eat with him might make me feel less rotten."

Anyhow, even though I'm sure Ma knew that something was up, she didn't ask a lot of questions, just said I could come.

Luckily, when we got there, there was no one I knew at the restaurant, so I wasn't that self-conscious about walking to our seats. Also, it helped that we ended up in a booth all the way in the corner, where the most anyone could see of me was the back of my head. That's usually the best you can expect when you're eating in public with your family.

When the waitress came, Ma ordered Skelly a short stack of pancakes with strawberries and whipped cream on top.

Skelly has an unbelievable sweet tooth these days. You should have seen his face when his order finally came. He started grinning ear to ear, like this was the best morning of his life.

It was one of those moments that can make you smile and break your heart at the same time.

I leaned over the table and cut up his breakfast for him. "Mmm. They look delicious, don't they, Skell? Mine do, too. See? I ordered the same thing you did."

Skelly put a forkful of food into his mouth. His face lit up all over again.

Already, he had whipped cream on his chin. I dipped my napkin in my glass of water and wiped it off, same as I always do at home.

I had just eaten my last bite of pancake when my mother pointed to Skelly's hands. "Syrup," she said. "Could you take him to the men's room and wash his hands?"

Slowly, I raised my eyes from my plate.

"*Excuse* me?" I asked.

I mean, what was she *thinking*? Hadn't I been a good enough grandson already this morning? Did she honestly expect me to walk across a room full of people holding Skelly's sticky hand?

"No, Ma. Geez. Come *on*," I said.

Right away, my mother stood up and reached for Skelly. "Fine. I'll take him to the men's room myself. Come on, Dad. This ought to be interesting."

Annoyed, I grabbed his hand away from her. "Okay, fine. I'll do it."

I waited until he was out of the booth, then pulled him along as fast as I could. Halfway across the room, he slowed down to look at some guy's French toast.

I jerked him away.

When we finally got inside the men's room, he waved at a bald man he didn't know.

Quick as I could, I rinsed and dried his hands with a paper towel. "There. You're done."

I opened the door and saw Ma in line at the cash register. Grabbing Skelly's hand again, I headed back across the floor. I was already figuring my strategy. I would take him straight to Ma, hand him off at the cash register, and wait for them outside.

It might have turned out okay, too. But when I was almost there, I caught a glimpse of two girls I knew standing in the waiting area. Felicia Dunn and Lea Falcone, two cheerleaders from my school.

I dropped Skelly's hand like a hot potato and lowered my head.

"Jake? Hey, Jake! Is that you?" called Felicia.

I picked up the pace. "No!" I blurted over my shoulder. "I mean, yeah, it's me. But I gotta go, okay? See ya."

Without ever looking up, I waved good-bye over my head. As I did, I tripped and fell into the door. I caught myself on the glass and turned to see if the girls had seen me. But instead, I saw Skelly.

My heart stopped.

He had done a U-turn and was heading back into the dining room.

I watched in horror as he stopped at the first table he came to and sat down. With a woman he didn't know.

He stared at her a second, then yelled, "Scat!"

The woman jumped up. "Manager! Somebody get the manager! This man is a nut!"

Ma ran right over.

I don't know what happened after that. I was already on my way to the car.

I knew the doors would be locked, but I tried them anyway, then took off walking. I crossed the parking lot and waited for the light to change. I was almost three blocks away when my mother and Skelly pulled up next to me.

She rolled down the passenger window and started to yell. "Excuse me, but did it ever occur to you to tell me you were walking home, Jake? Huh? Do you think I'm a mind reader? If it hadn't been for those two girls, Skelly and I would still be looking for you at the restaurant."

Great. Perfect. Now Felicia and Lea knew my grandfather was the nut.

Ma motioned to the backseat with her head. "Come on. Get in. We need to get home."

"I really want to walk." I sped up a little.

My mother did, too. "You're blowing this all out of proportion, Jake. What happened in the restaurant was no big deal, okay? As soon as I explained about the

Alzheimer's, the woman understood completely. She even offered Skelly a biscuit and jelly."

"Oh, gee, what a sweetheart." I kept going.

My mother's voice got more impatient. "Get in, please. *Now*. You know I've got to go to work."

"But you said you called Mrs. Russell to stay with Skelly."

"I did. But—"

Just then, a horn honked.

I looked around. Ma was driving so slow, three cars were backed up behind her.

The guy laid on his horn again.

My mother stuck her head out the window and yelled for him to "keep his drawers on."

That did it. I turned and started running in the opposite direction. I cut through a shopping center and under a fence. Ten minutes later, I was standing in my school parking lot.

At the other end, facing me head-on, was the Dumpster.

I stopped to catch my breath. Then, slowly, I walked to it and looked over the top.

Empty paint cans. That's what Skelly had gone in there to get. They had been repainting the inside of the gym, getting it ready for graduation, and the bottom of the Dumpster was filled with empty paint cans and used brushes and rollers. It's weird that Skelly's still so fascinated by that kind of stuff. But whenever he sees paint cans, his brain makes some sort of weird connection with his past, and he can't seem to let it go.

I sat down on the asphalt. It was warm on my legs. I closed my eyes and leaned my back against the side of the bin.

My mind went back to the restaurant and how completely Ma had misunderstood why I'd taken off. Did she honest-to-God think I cared that she'd smoothed things over with some shrieky old woman? Did it not even *dawn* on her that two popular cheerleaders from school had watched my grandfather put on a public performance of "The Nut."

"BUD! HEY, BUD! IS THAT YOU?"

The high-pitched voice sounded like fingernails on a chalkboard.

There's only one person in the universe who has a voice like that.

I opened one eye.

Mrs. Russell.

On nice days she walks to our house. The school parking lot is a shortcut.

I scrunched myself together and hid my face in my knees.

"OH, NO YOU DON'T! DON'T YOU GO HIDING YOUR HEAD AND PRETENDING YOU DON'T SEE ME!"

I waited for the *ha*. Whenever Mrs. Russell says something she thinks is hilarious, she almost always follows it up with this loud—

"HA!"

Even though it was clear that I wanted to be left alone, Mrs. Russell kept walking toward me. I could hear her getting closer. Not her footsteps. Her *stockings*. You'd be amazed at how far away the human ear can detect the sound of legs swishing together in those heavy white nurse's stockings. Bill Nye the Science Guy should do a show on it.

Swish . . . swish . . . swish . . . SWISH . . . SWISH . . .

Finally, I gave up and raised my head.

"Aha! I knew it was you, Bud!"

She calls me Bud.

"What're you doing down there, anyway?" she squawked. "What's wrong with you?"

Except when she talks to Skelly, Mrs. Russell's voice can puncture a truck tire.

"Nothing, Mrs. Russell. I'm just sitting here by myself. You know . . . being *alone*."

I stressed the *alone* part as much as I could. But Mrs. Russell bent over at the waist and leaned closer to my face. "Are you sure nothing's wrong? It's not Skelly, is it, Jake? Your mother didn't mention anything was wrong."

"That's because nothing *is* wrong," I told her. "Skelly's fine, Mrs. Russell."

She still looked doubtful. "Really and truly?"

"Yes. Really and truly."

You could see her relax. "Whew. That's good," she said.

Then—without any warning at all—she reached out and grabbed my nose.

"Honk! Honk!"

I should have known it was coming. To Mrs. Russell, honking someone's nose is the height of comedy. She thinks it's a real mood lifter.

After she did it, I was afraid she would just keep standing there, trying to shoot the breeze. But instead, she stood straight up and looked at her watch. "Lord save us! I told your mother I would be there by ten fifteen. If I don't leave now, she'll be late to work."

Then, quick as anything, she took off swishing again.

She was halfway to the gate when she turned around again. "Hey, Bud! When you get home, maybe you and me can get your grandpop to take a bath!" she screeched.

Across the parking lot, two guys were on their way to ball practice. They cracked up like you wouldn't believe.

I hid my face again.

It was becoming a way of life.

When I finally went home that morning, Mrs. Russell and Skelly were sitting on the front-porch steps. Skelly was eating a Fudgsicle.

In the summertime, he almost always has a Fudgsicle in the morning. My grandfather loves chocolate even more than pancakes with whipped cream and strawberries.

As soon as he saw me, he stopped licking his ice cream and smiled.

"Claude Harper!" he said.

It made me laugh, the way he said it. Like he was just plain happy to see me. Whoever I was.

I stopped on the step and ruffled his hair.

"Got yourself a Fudgsicle, huh, Skell? Man, your sweet tooth is having a blast this morning, isn't it?"

Mrs. Russell stood up.

"Could you stay out here with him for a second, Bud? He just dropped an ice-cream bar in the kitchen and it's melting all over the floor."

I told her okay and sat down next to him. A drip of chocolate ice cream fell onto his hand.

"Whoa, it's starting to melt, Skell. You've gotta eat it faster, okay?"

I picked up the paper towel Mrs. Russell had left and cleaned him up.

After I finished, Skelly's eyes drifted away and he stared into space.

When he finally looked at me again, his face seemed puzzled. "Have you seen my mother? Is my mother coming home today?" he asked.

I put my arm around his shoulder. "I don't know, Skell," I said. "I haven't seen your mother today. I don't really think she's coming, though."

I paused a second and softened my voice. "Today, I think you'll just stay here with me."

7

The Pearl

Eighth-grade graduation was three weeks away. I can't really say I was getting in the spirit of it, though. When you haven't felt like you're part of the class for a while, the thought of graduating and moving on doesn't really choke you up that much.

Still, that doesn't mean there weren't good things about it, because there definitely were. The best thing was how some of my teachers had already eased up on homework and stuff. I mean, there are certain teachers who just get it, you know? They understand that kids' brains go on vacation the first week in May. And that no matter how hard you knock, there won't be anyone home until September.

Take my English teacher, Mr. Bork, for instance. I had an oral book report due on May 19. But since my brain was already on vacation, I couldn't get myself motivated. So on the day it was due, I told Bork that something "kind of serious" had come up at home, and I wasn't quite ready to give the report.

60

Mr. Bork, who was grading papers at the time, didn't even look up from his desk. "Haven't read the book yet, have you, Mr. Moon?" he asked.

I shook my head. "Not a word."

For some reason, that made him smile, and he told me, "One more week."

Seriously. The guy was so understanding, I should have asked if we could just call off the whole thing.

The thing is, I'm not a big fan of the oral book report. In my opinion, an oral book report doesn't benefit society in any way. The class hates listening to it as much as you hate giving it. Trust me, if anyone in your class ever looks amused while you're giving an oral book report, it's because your zipper is down.

Anyhow, since Bork gave me an extra week, I put it off for three more days before I even thought about it again. Finally though, on Sunday, I dug the book out of my backpack and started to read.

The Pearl, by John Steinbeck. It was a nice title, I thought. An oyster story was what I was thinking. But even if it was boring, it was only 118 pages, so how could I go wrong?

I'll tell you how I could go wrong.

By *reading* it.

The Pearl started out depressing and went downhill from there. I began reading at noon and didn't finish till after six. I could have read it faster, but every couple of chapters I had to stop and throw it across the room.

To put it mildly, *The Pearl* is a book without hope.

Something good happens in the beginning, and then right away everything starts going wrong. And it keeps going wronger and wronger, until you don't even want to turn the page hardly, 'cause you know how much wronger it's still going to get.

And here's what I hated most of all. I identified with it, so close you wouldn't believe. Because for me, that's exactly how Skelly's Alzheimer's has felt. From the first day he found out he had it, everything in our life has gone steadily downhill. And no matter how hard I try, all I can see in front of us are more sad pages.

But still, I have to admit, every single time I threw *The Pearl* across the room, I always went over and picked it up again. I guess something inside of me just needed to know that even in a story as miserable as this one, things could end up okay. Not rip-roaringly happy, maybe. But okay.

And so I read it all the way to the end.

And a baby got shot.

I swear, I'm not making that up. That's how John Steinbeck ended his book. Do you call that creative writing? Does it really take a lot of imagination to end a story by killing a baby, do you think?

A few minutes after I threw the book across the room for the last time, I heard Aunt Marguerite and James come in the front door. I looked at my clock and saw it was six thirty. Time for Sunday dinner together.

I groaned. Not *James*. Not *now*.

Eating dinner with James had become one of the most

dreaded parts of my week. James may be older than me, but he has no scruples. Not even one. Which is not to say that I'm overflowing with scruples, myself. But no matter how low I go, James goes even lower.

Like a couple of months ago, while we were eating, he asked me to pass him a roll. And so just to be nice, I warmed it up under my armpit for a few seconds. Which even now makes me bust out laughing. Except right away, James responded by licking his thumb and sticking it in the middle of my mashed potatoes. He said he was constructing a *holding pond* for my gravy. And keep in mind that the kid is in high school, okay? But that's how childish he still is. And unsanitary.

Anyhow, because of Skelly's condition, Family Night dinner is almost always at our house. Aunt Marguerite and Ma take turns fixing the food. When it's my mother's turn, she cooks a roast or a chicken. When it's Aunt Marguerite's turn, she carries in two bags of Chinese food and plops them on the table.

If my aunt wrote a cookbook, it would be called *Order Out*.

"Jake! Dinner! Come on, let's go!" Ma shouted. "Chinese tonight!"

I didn't want to go. I was already in a terrible mood, and watching James cram his mouth full of sweet-and-sour pork would make me suicidal.

Ma waited a couple of minutes, then came to get me.

"Hey, you. Didn't you hear me calling? Everyone's at the table waiting for you. The food is getting cold. Let's go."

"I can't, Ma. I need to finish this book report. I'll eat later, okay? Just this once?"

The Pearl was lying on the floor near the door. My mother stared down at it.

"It fell off the bed," I said.

"And did what?" she asked. "Flew across the room?"

"It's a light book."

She picked it up. "*The Pearl.* Hmm. I think I read this in high school, but I can't remember the story."

"Oh, be*lieeeve* me, Ma. If you'd ever read *The Pearl,* you wouldn't have forgotten the story. It's about this poor fisherman who finds a pearl the size of a baseball. And so he and his wife are totally happy for about a page and a half. And then all this terrible stuff starts to happen to him. And at the end, their baby gets shot. It's a real rib tickler."

My mother tossed it on the bed. "Then what you need is to get away from it for a while. Come on, Jake. It's Family Night. You can come back and finish your report right after dinner. You won't even have to help me with the dishes. I promise."

She took my hand and pulled me off the bed.

As she dragged me into the dining room, Aunt Marguerite blew me a kiss from the table.

I waved halfheartedly.

James never looked up from his plate. A couple of cartons of food were stuffed in his mouth already.

I patted his shoulder as I sat down next to him. "Thank you for waiting, James," I said. "Really, though. You should have started without me."

James kept eating like I was invisible.

Across from me, Skelly had started eating, too. The corners of his mouth had already collected bits of egg roll, and there were two pieces of rice stuck to his chin.

Even though Aunt Marguerite was sitting right next to him, she didn't make a move to clean his face.

If I had been in a better mood, I probably would have just reached over and flicked them off with my finger. Instead though, I got up deliberately slow, walked all around the table, and dabbed at his mouth with my napkin.

Aunt Marguerite looked embarrassed. "Oh, I'm sorry, Jake. I could have done that," she said.

I didn't say "that's okay" or anything. Just walked back to my seat.

Meanwhile, James had still not raised his head. He was hunkered over his dinner like he was protecting it from an alien invasion.

As soon as I sat down again, Aunt Marguerite started acting all friendly and chatty. "So, Jake. You were back there doing homework, huh?"

I nodded. "Yup."

"What kind of homework?" she asked.

"A book report."

"On what?"

"A book."

Ma kicked me under the table.

"*The Pearl*," I said.

"*The Pearl*," she repeated. "Didn't you read that last year, James? It seems to me you read that one."

"I doubt it," I said. "It's not a sticker book."

Without moving his head, James rolled his eyes to the side to look at me. Under his breath, he called me a foul name.

I gasped in pretend shock.

"Ummmmm," I said loudly. "Did anyone hear that? James called me a naughty word at Family Night dinner."

Ma threw her head back in frustration.

"Please. Could we please just finish our food in peace for once? Would that be okay with you guys? Could you just put a lid on it for the rest of the meal?"

James shrugged and went right back to his plate. He must have been especially hungry, or he never would have given up that easily.

As usual, the minute he and Aunt Marguerite finished eating, they got Skelly up from the table and headed for the door. As soon as dinner is over, they always whisk him outside for their weekly stroll around the block.

Aunt Marguerite calls it their "quality time" together.

I call it "Aunt Marguerite's Totally Lame Excuse to Get Out of Doing the Dishes." It's a miracle how she always gets back just as Ma is starting the dishwasher.

The part I love best, though, is how my aunt wraps up the evening each week. When she comes back in the door after their walk, she puts Skelly in his recliner and goes straight to her purse. Then she pulls out her big, fat checkbook and writes Ma a check for Mrs. Russell's salary.

She always waves the check around in the air after she fills it out, too. Like she's helping the ink dry. Then she takes the check over to my mother and presents it to her like she's one of those guys from the Prize Patrol.

"Five hundred dollars," she announces. As if from week to week Ma forgets what Mrs. Russell's salary is.

After that, everyone hugs, except me and James. And then *poof!* My aunt and my cousin are back in their car, driving across town. Where they are magically transformed into normal, regular people with no sad old man to take care of.

On this particular night, I stood at the door watching Aunt Marguerite's lights disappear down the street. From the living room, I could hear Skelly clapping along with the contestants on *Wheel of Fortune*. He can't solve the puzzles, but he's totally into the clapping.

I glanced in at him as I started back down the hall.

My mother was sitting on the couch. She shot me an annoyed look. "You could have done better at dinner," she growled.

I stopped. "What? What did I do?"

She got up from the couch and met me in the doorway. "You know perfectly well what you did, Jake. It wasn't enough that you had to make a huge production out of wiping Skelly's face. Oh, no. Then you had to throw in all those smart-alecky remarks about the book report."

"I was kidding, Ma," I said.

"No, you weren't. You know you weren't," she said. "Family Night is supposed to be about all of us spending time together with Skelly. But lately it's been nothing but a battle of insults between you and James.

And I'm telling you right now, it has got to stop."

"Good. Fine. Let's stop it, then," I said. "If you want me in a better mood, then stop having James and Aunt Marguerite over to dinner every Sunday. And please, Ma, don't tell me one more time about how Family Night is supposed to be about Skelly. I know that perfectly well, okay? But in case you haven't noticed, Aunt Marguerite can't even stand to *touch* Skelly. And so what kind of great family do you call that?"

My voice got louder. "Oh yeah. And you can talk all you want about me wiping that rice off his face. But you *know* Aunt Marguerite saw it, Ma. She just didn't want to get her hands dirty by touching him. Skelly could be sitting there with a cream pie on his head, and Aunt Marguerite wouldn't lift a finger."

"That's not true," said my mother. "Marguerite is just as concerned about taking care of your—"

Something inside me exploded.

"NO, SHE'S NOT, MOTHER! She's not one bit concerned about taking care of him. She's concerned that *other people* take care of him. Namely, you and me. Why can't you see that? She eats with him once a week to make herself feel better. And then she writes us a big la-di-da check. And she and James go home to their la-di-da wonderful life."

Ma threw her hands in the air. "So what do you suggest that I do? Huh? You want me to shuffle the poor old man back and forth between our houses so his disease will punish us all equally? The money Marguerite gives us is important. The money is *huge*. Without your aunt's money, Skelly would be in a nursing home somewhere. And in case you've forgotten, this is his home. And he deserves to live here as long he can."

She ran her fingers through her hair. "Good Lord, Jake. You, above everyone else, should know how much we owe—"

I covered my ears. "I know, Ma. I know, I know. I've heard this part a billion times. We owe him, we owe him, we owe him."

My throat burned from trying not to cry. "I'm doing the best I can right now, okay? I'm *trying*. But God, Mother. I'm fourteen years old. And I'm a caregiver to an old man who thinks I'm Claude Harper."

Suddenly, Skelly stood up and started tugging on his slacks.

Ma saw him from the doorway and ran in. She grabbed his hand and hurried him to the bathroom.

I waited to make sure everything was okay, then started to my bedroom again.

Ma passed me in the hall and reached for my hand.

"I don't want to fight with you, Jake," she said. "I just want to have a peaceful meal on Sunday. But I'm not the enemy here. You and I are in this together. And no one understands how God-awful hard Skelly's disease has been on you better than I do."

Her voice cracked a little. "I carry the guilt of that with me every single day. And if being bitter and resentful would make your life happier, I swear I'd tell you to go for it. But believe me, Jake, staying bitter will only make you more miserable."

She paused then, and I know she was hoping I'd hug her. I couldn't though.

Instead, I took my hand away.

"*More* miserable?" I said quietly. "More is pretty hard to imagine, Ma."

I stepped around her and kept on walking.

8

Sinking and Floating

On Wednesday morning, I was already awake when I heard the alarm go off in Ma's bedroom.

A few minutes later, she called to me from across the hall. "Jake? You up yet?"

I rolled over and looked at the calendar on my desk. May 26. The day my book report was due.

English was fifth period, and I still hadn't finished my notes on *The Pearl*. It's against Mr. Bork's rules to read your book report from a piece of paper. But at least he lets you use note cards.

Ma opened my door. "Come on, you. Get up. It's six thirty already."

I yawned and got out of bed.

The daily routine had begun.

Every morning while my mother takes her shower, I get Skelly out of bed and point him to the bathroom. After he's done, I help him wash his hands and face. Then we head back to his room to get ready for the *real* fun. Dressing him.

These days my grandfather's wardrobe is mostly T-shirts and pants with elastic waistbands, so normally it goes pretty fast. But on this particular morning, his easy clothes were in the hamper. So Ma had laid out a shirt with buttons. And regular pants, with a zipper.

I took a few deep breaths to get myself ready. "Okay, Skell. Let's give it a shot."

He sat down on his bed and we maneuvered his feet into his pant legs. Then he stood again, so I could pull them up. But before they were all the way to his waist, he was already yanking on the zipper.

"No, Skell, wait. If you zip up too soon, you always get your boxers jammed in a big—"

He gave a hard tug.

I looked down.

"—wad," I added quietly.

This time, the boxers were stuck so tight, the zipper wouldn't move in either direction. While I worked to get it free, Skelly started fastening his shirt. It takes him forever to do a button these days. And even when he's successful, it's almost always in the wrong hole.

When I finally got everything unstuck and buttoned, he was sitting on the edge of the bed again, ready for his shoes and socks. Just for the record, my grandfather will only wear red socks. If you put any other color socks on him, he'll take them off during the day and put them in the kitchen sink.

After I helped him into his shoes, he leaned over and fastened the Velcro.

I gave him a thumbs-up. "Excellent job with the Velcro this morning, Skell," I said.

It was already later than usual, so I hurried him out to the kitchen. Skelly and I have been eating breakfast together every morning since I was a baby. Our roles are totally reversed now, but still, I consider it a tradition.

He sat down at the table and I poured his orange juice. He drank it while I got his Cheerios. It's been his favorite cereal for almost a year. He likes trying to sink the *o*'s with his spoon.

As soon as I put the bowl in front of him, he asked the same question he always asks.

"What's this?"

"Cheerios," I told him. "They're Cheerios, Skell. You like them."

I poured his milk.

He tried to sink them with his spoon.

"They float," he said.

"Yeah, they do."

He took a bite. "Mmm."

I nodded and ate a couple of bites of my own cereal.

By then, Skelly was staring down into his bowl again.

"What's this?"

"Cheerios, Skell. They're Cheerios."

"They float."

"Yeah, they do."

"Mmm."

Last year, when he first started this routine, I thought he was just being lazy. I thought he wasn't even *trying* to remember. So when he asked what they were for the fifth time, I totally lost it.

"Cheerios, Skelly!" I hollered. "Now, don't ask me that one more time, and I mean it! Nobody's brain can be that fried! Not even yours."

I grabbed his bowl away from him.

"I *know* you can remember the name of this cereal. I'm positive you can. Just tell me the name, and I'll give it right back."

He sat there.

"I'm not kidding around, Skelly. You're not getting this back until you tell me the name. Now *think*, okay? What did I say it was? What? What? What?"

My grandfather's eyes started to well up.

"Oh, no, Skelly. Please don't cry. I'm sorry, okay?"

I quick put the bowl back in front of him.

"Look. See? Here's your cereal back. *Cheerios,* Skelly. Its name is *Cheerios.*"

I dried his eyes with his napkin and hugged him as tight as I could.

"Morning, Bud!"

Skelly had just started his cereal when Mrs. Russell came rushing through the front door. She has her own key to our house, so she always comes in without knocking. Since August, she's caught me in my underwear four times. All four times she's started singing "I See London, I See France."

I looked at the clock. It was a little before seven.

Usually, Mrs. Russell doesn't come till after I'm gone.

"What's going on? Why are you so early this morning?" I asked her.

She came over and gave Skelly's arm a pat. "Because me and your sweet grandpop here have a date for the pancake breakfast at the Senior Center," she said.

Then, in a flash, she snatched his cereal bowl right out from under his nose.

"Whoops. Can't be eating cereal this morning, Skelly fella," she told him. "We've gotta save room for those delicious blueberry flapjacks."

I waited for Skelly to start pitching a fit about his missing Cheerios. But Mrs. Russell had him up and out of the chair before he even realized they were gone.

I left the two of them together in the kitchen and went to take my shower.

Fifteen minutes later, I was turning off the water when I heard the front door shut. I took my towel and wiped a circle in the foggy bathroom window. Through the steam, I watched Mrs. Russell take a hold of Skelly's hand and trot him across the street.

When they got to the other side, she knelt down and pulled up his red socks. He leaned his hand on her shoulder for support. Before she stood back up, she smoothed his pant legs nice and neat. Then she held his hand again, gave it another pat, and they went on down the block.

Ma banged on the bathroom door. "Hurry up, Jake! It's seven fifteen! You're going to be late!"

My mother announces the time more often than Big

Ben. I don't know why she won't get off my back about being late. In nine years of school, I've never been late one time.

As usual, I got to school in plenty of time before the bell. Unfortunately, though, I still didn't have my notes done for my book report. So at noon, I had to skip lunch and go to the library.

The notes finally got done. But my stomach didn't get fed. And by the time the bell rang for fifth period, it was growling so loud I swear it was echoing off the lockers in the hall.

I stopped at the water fountain and drank all I could. But when I finally sat down at my desk in English, the growling had gotten even louder.

I started to panic. I mean, it's not like this book report wasn't already stressful enough without adding body noises into the mix.

To try to muffle the sound, I bent in half and pretended to be searching through my backpack on the floor.

I was still down there when Mr. Bork began taking role. He couldn't see me and called my name. "Mr. Moon?"

I was seriously considering not answering, when a noise suddenly exploded from the hall.

ERRNNTTT! ERRNNTTT! ERRNNTTT!

Oh, my God! I couldn't believe it!

A fire drill! It was a fire drill!

I was saved by the bell!

I'm *never* that lucky. Never, ever, ever!

And as it turned out, that wasn't the end of my good luck, either. Because there was a huge traffic jam in the hall, it took an extra-long time for all the classes to get out of the building. Plus, once we were out there, Mr. Bork and Mr. Treacher, the science teacher, got so involved in a conversation that even after we came back in, they kept talking in the doorway for at least another ten minutes.

So as amazing as this sounds, when Bork finally got back to his desk, he looked at the clock and told me he was sorry, but there were other things he needed to get to. And there wouldn't be time for my book report.

"Okay if we try again next week sometime, Mr. Moon?" he asked.

I lowered my head in this kind of hangdog look I do sometimes. "Yeah, well . . . I guess so," I said.

I should be an actor. Seriously. Academy Awards have been given out for performances worse than that one.

9

Officer Happy

At the end of the day, I came out of school feeling euphoric. *Euphoric* was a vocabulary word this year. According to the dictionary, it means "feeling great happiness." But what *euphoric* really means is that if no one was watching, you would skip home.

As I started up my street, I honestly thought that my day couldn't get any better. But when I raised my head and saw a cop car parked in front of our neighbors the Waxmans', my mouth fell all the way open.

I'd always suspected that the cops would come for Mr. Waxman one day. But for it to happen on the day of my book report miracle . . . well, it was almost more luck than one kid deserved.

I sped up. There was no way I was going to miss this.

I mean, you can tell just by looking at Mr. Waxman that he's on the shady side of the law. For one thing, he wears a hat. Not a baseball cap. A *man's* hat. With a brim and all.

And not only that, but he's got one of those creepy, thin mustaches that looks like he draws it on with a pencil. Which is a crime in itself, if you ask me.

But what *really* makes Mr. Waxman suspicious is the way he never opens the door all the way when I knock. Like even when I'm standing there holding a package that got delivered to my house by mistake, Mr. Waxman will only open the door wide enough to peek one eye out. Then, in a move so fast it's like a blur, he reaches out, snatches the box out of my hands, and shuts the door right in my face.

A second later, the door opens another crack, and he says, "Think-Q." Which I'm pretty sure is supposed to be "thank you."

I hurried even more. I was hoping I hadn't missed the part where they put him in the back of the squad car and hold his head down so he won't bump it.

"Whoops. Watch the old hat there, Mr. W.," I'd say.

I laughed out loud. In fact, just to show you what a good mood I was in, even when I got close enough to realize that the cop car was in front of *my* house and not the Waxmans', it still didn't register that anything was actually wrong.

I walked inside. The cop was standing in the kitchen. Ma and Mrs. Russell were sitting at the table, looking through the pages of our photo albums.

Weird, I thought. Why would a cop want to look at our family pictures?

My mother glanced up. "Oh . . . Jake," she said absentmindedly. Then her eyes went right back to the album.

"Ma?"

All of a sudden, she pointed at one of the pictures. "Here!" she said to the cop. "This is the one I was telling you about. Look, see? It's a close-up just like I said. It was taken this past December."

She pulled it out of the plastic and handed it to him.

I was seriously starting not to like this.

"Mother?"

Just then, Ma's hand went over her mouth as if she were seeing me for the first time. "Oh, God, Jake. I'm sorry. You don't know yet . . . It's your grandfather," she said. "He walked away from the Senior Center this morning."

For a second, I was speechless.

"What? But . . . but *how*, Ma? I mean, how is that even possible? They've got an alarm on every door at that place. And besides, I thought Mrs. Russell stays with him over there."

Mrs. Russell put her head on the table and muttered, "Dear Lord."

Ma reached for her hand. "Alma does stay with him, Jake. But today when they got there, some men were painting the outside of the building, and Skelly wanted to watch. And then Alma mentioned to them that he used to be a painter and—"

"They told him he could help," Mrs. Russell interrupted. "They said if it was okay with the people inside, it was okay with them. And then one of the painters gave him some white overalls and a hat to put on. And he said he'd keep an eye on Skelly while I ran inside to check with the program supervisor."

She covered her face and shook her head. "I was only gone a couple of minutes, Bud. But the man didn't know much about Alzheimer's, I guess. Because he got distracted mixing some paint, and when he turned around again, Skelly was gone."

Ma stood up. "We're going to get him back soon though. Right, Officer?" she said. "I mean, how hard can it be to find an old man in white painter's overalls and an ID necklace?"

I still don't know if the cop was planning to answer. But if he was, he didn't do it fast enough to please my mother.

"Excuse me. . . . *Sir?* I don't mean to be rude. But would it kill you to give us a little encouragement here?"

The cop looked tired. He said they would do their best.

"So who's looking for him now?" I asked. "Right this minute, I mean. Is anyone out there at all?"

My mother nodded. "Four or five volunteers from the Senior Center have been driving around all day. And Aunt Marguerite's been looking, too. Right now she's picking up James from school, and the two of them are going to keep searching."

Without another word, I flew out the front door and took off running.

If anyone could find Skelly, I could. I'd start from the Senior Center and figure out where to go from there.

I was only a block from the building when the patrol car pulled up next to me.

It was the same cop who Ma had yelled at. He rolled down the window. "I told your mother I'd come get you. There's a lot of area to cover, kid. And there's no sense having you and your grandfather both lost."

I started backing up. "No. I can find him. I swear. I know all his favorite shortcuts around here."

I pointed across the street. "See that alley over there? On Saturdays, when we'd go fishing at the park, we would always cut through that alley. Nobody knows that kind of stuff but me."

It took all the nerve I had, but I walked away.

I had only gone a few yards when the cop pulled up next to me again. He opened the passenger-side door.

"Okay, how 'bout this? You get in the car, and I'll let you ride with me for a while."

"Yeah, good, thanks," I said, then I ran around the back and slid into the front seat.

The car smelled like BO and cigarettes. Also, the side window was smeary with fingerprints. Through the glass, the world looked smudged and dirty.

The cop picked up his walkie-talkie thing and told someone to call my mother. "Tell her I have the kid with me and we're looking for the old man."

The kid and the old man. Real nice. That's how police officers refer to you when they're not on their best behavior being taped for *Cops.*

After he hung up, he asked, "Which way?"

I pointed to the alley again, and he turned.

We were almost to the other end when he yawned. His mouth opened so wide it could have held a bowling ball. Like he was so bored to tears with this whole stupid assignment, he could hardly keep his eyes open.

It really bothered me that he did that.

"He's worth your time, if that's what you're wondering," I said. "He's not just some crazy old man."

The cop stopped the car.

"Look, kid, let's get something straight. I'm happy to look for your grandfather, okay? I *want* to look for your grandfather. In fact, my shift was over an hour ago, and I *volunteered* to look for your grandfather. But I've been up since four o'clock this morning, so if you and your mother were expecting Officer Happy, you're flat out of luck today."

He looked over at me and raised his eyebrows. "We clear?"

I squirmed uncomfortably in my seat and nodded.

I was just about to turn my eyes back to the window when I glanced down and saw his gun. It was right there in his holster, not two feet away from my hand.

I don't like guns.

Skelly hated them.

I stared at the black handle of the gun and remembered the terrible ending of *The Pearl*.

A chill ran through my body. What if John Steinbeck turned out to be right? What if there are some people in the world who just aren't meant to be happy? People whose lives just keep getting worse and worse until they finally hit bottom, and nothing can hurt them anymore?

I tried to push the thought out of my mind.

Turning back to the window, I looked through the smudge marks.

We drove on.

10

Sherman Kelly

It was after dark when I finally got home.

Aunt Marguerite and James were sitting at the table with Ma. Mrs. Russell was standing at the back-door window, staring outside. There were bags of burgers and fries on the table, but nobody was eating. Not even James.

All four looked at me. I shook my head no.

Ma stood up and hugged me. "Don't worry, we'll find him."

She crossed her fingers and looked at Aunt Marguerite. "Maybe even tonight, huh? After the news."

My aunt crossed her fingers back.

I didn't get it. "What do you mean? What's the news got to do with anything?"

With her fingers still crossed, my mother pointed at Marguerite. "Your aunt just got back from the TV station downtown. She took Dad's picture to the station manager, and the woman promised to show it on the ten o'clock news tonight."

Suddenly, I felt hopeful. "That's good, Aunt Marguerite."

She smiled a little.

"No, I mean that's *really* good," I told her. "Why didn't I think of that?"

James smirked. "Because the brains of the family thought of it first," he said. "That would be me."

"Yeah, right. Sure you did, Einstein."

"No, seriously. I did. Why would I lie?"

I laughed out loud. "Gee, I don't know, James. Maybe because you wouldn't know the truth if it came right up and bit you on the—"

My mother stood up so fast her chair fell over behind her. "Do not start, Jake! I mean it! Don't you dare start this stuff now!" Then she pushed the chair out of the way with her foot and hurried out of the room.

Aunt Marguerite narrowed her eyes. "Thank you both so very much. This is just exactly what we needed," she said. Then she left, too.

For a few seconds, James tapped his fingers on the table. "Well, we're all pulling together nicely," he said dryly. After that, he drifted out the door to watch TV.

I sat down in his chair and put my head in my hands. I don't know how long I stayed there—at least a couple of minutes, probably.

"Mercy."

My skin prickled when I heard her voice. Don't ask me how, but I'd managed to forget that Mrs. Russell was still in the room.

I frowned. Why, though? Why *was* she still in the room? She wasn't a member of the family. And we sure as heck didn't need an audience watching us fall apart. Especially not the person who was responsible for losing Skelly in the first place.

I stood up and spun around. "I think you need to go now, Mrs. Russell."

She looked surprised. "But . . . but your mother said I could stay until—"

"Yeah, well Ma's not feeling too good now, okay?"

I handed her her purse from off the counter. "Here. I'll walk you to your car."

I took her arm and led her outside.

When we got to the porch, she started to sniffle. "Everyone's mad at me," she said.

I didn't argue.

At the top of the step, she stopped and blew her nose. It sounded like the honk of a wild goose.

Her car was a big old clunker of a thing. As I opened the heavy driver-side door, it swung wide and stuck on the edge of the curb.

Slowly, Mrs. Russell came down the sidewalk. When she got in the car, she hunched forward slightly and leaned her head on the steering wheel.

The horn honked loudly.

Honest to God. The woman was a human honk machine.

I couldn't stay there one more second. I turned and hurried back inside.

Fifteen minutes later, she was still out there. I had been hoping to outlast her. But my anger was fading and I couldn't hold on.

I went outside to the curb again.

"No one's mad at you, okay, Mrs. Russell? We're just tired, that's all. We're just beat."

I lifted the car door from its stuck position. But before I closed it, I bent down. "Come back in the morning, okay? We really want you to."

She took my hand and patted it.

I didn't pull away.

For the next three hours, Ma and Aunt Marguerite talked in the bedroom. If you walked down the hall, you could hear their voices, all hushed and low, coming through the bottom of the door.

James and I were watching TV in the living room when the clock on the wall started to chime. I looked up. Eight o'clock. The time when we usually asked Skelly if he needed to use the bathroom.

I closed my eyes. "Great. What's he gonna do tonight?"

James looked over. "What?"

"Nothing. Never mind. It's just that we usually remind Skelly to pee around now, that's all."

James looked curious. "Remind him? Why do you need to remind him? How can a person forget to pee? Even a three-year-old can tell when he has to—"

"Hey, James? Just take my word on this one, okay? He's forgotten before. That's all I'm saying."

"Okay, fine. He's forgotten," he said. "I just didn't know."

He went over to the window and pulled back the curtains. "I do know one thing for sure. It's pitch-black dark out tonight."

He leaned his face closer to the glass. "God, there's no moon at all, hardly."

I glared at him. "Here's an idea, James. Why don't you try to make me even *more* sick about this than I already am?"

Suddenly—with no warning at all—James came charging at me from across the room. When he got to my chair, he shoved me in the shoulders with both hands.

"Hey! Knock it off!" I said.

"Shut up!" he said. "Just shut up, Jake. What is it with you, anyway? Why is everything always about *you* and *your* feelings? Why is it okay for you to worry me with all that stuff about Skelly's bathroom problems, but as soon as I say it's dark . . . *bam!* It's all about poor little Jake and his sensitive feelings."

He shoved my shoulders again. "You think *I'm* not worried? Huh? You think I'm some jerk who doesn't love his own grandfather? I get the picture, okay? You're the favorite grandson. That's always been made crystal clear. But that doesn't mean I don't love him just as much as you do."

He flopped down on the couch again and started clicking through the channels with the remote.

A second later, he brushed his hands across his eyes.

He probably didn't think I saw that, but I did.

I left the room and went to the kitchen until my breathing calmed.

A couple of minutes later, I started for my room. I slowed as I passed the living-room door, and muttered, "Sorry."

I'm not sure if James heard me. But at least I said it.

Sometimes I'm wrong.

Not that often.

But it happens.

Ma came in to get me around ten. The news was about to start, and she wanted all of us to watch it together.

James didn't look at me when I walked back in. He and Marguerite were sitting on the couch, and he turned his eyes away.

We had to wait for almost twenty minutes for the story about Skelly to come on. The first time they broke away for commercials, the newswoman used Skelly as a teaser.

"Coming up . . . a local family needs your help in finding a missing loved one," she said.

But when she came back, instead of the story on Skelly, she did an in-depth report on a farmer who grew a squash that looked like a baseball bat.

More commercials. Then the weather.

Finally, when they came back from their millionth commercial break, Skelly's picture was in a little box in the top corner of the TV screen. It was the same picture Ma had given the cop that afternoon.

The newswoman's face went from smiling to serious in warp speed.

"We have a sad story for you now," she said. "Earlier

this morning, a local Alzheimer's patient wandered away from the Northeast Senior Center at 1750 Maple Avenue."

The camera zoomed in on Skelly's face.

"The police are asking for your help in finding this gentleman," she said. "He answers to the name of Sherman Kelly."

James jumped up. "No, he doesn't!"

All of us stared in disbelief as the woman moved on to the next story.

She was already smiling again.

11

Candle Burns

I sat up the whole night with the lights on. I didn't even get under my covers.

It just seemed fair to do that, I thought. When your grandfather is wandering around all night in the darkness, it seems sort of selfish to sleep through it, all safe and sound.

I napped off and on the next day. I'd already told Ma that I wasn't going to school until we found Skelly, and she hadn't argued. When he still hadn't turned up by Thursday night, I sat up then, too. I took a cold shower at 2 A.M. and another one at quarter to five.

On Friday morning, I was the tiredest I'd ever been in my life.

Also, the cleanest.

Friday night around six, I fell asleep on the couch eating a chopped sirloin TV dinner. Ma covered me up with an afghan and let me sleep.

I didn't wake up until almost nine o'clock the next

morning. That's when some idiot started pressing on our front-door buzzer.

It's not healthy being scared awake by a door buzzer. It gets your heart rhythms totally out of whack. I was still trying to get my breathing under control when I heard Ma say, "Come in."

I was sure it was Mrs. Russell. She'd been coming over every morning since Skelly had disappeared. This time she must have forgotten her key.

I pulled the afghan over my head and tried to fall back to sleep. I'd been having a dream and I wanted to get back to it.

It had been about Skelly. He'd been wandering around in this huge, sandy desert. But right before I woke up, I was pretty sure he had spotted an oasis.

I tried to put the pieces together. If the dream was about the desert, maybe I was worried that Skelly didn't have any water to drink. I've read that a person can only go a few days without water. But then again, you can't really die of thirst in a city, can you?

The thought bothered me.

Why can't you? Like if an old man is confused and scared—and he hardly even talks—where does he go to get a drink? Who will give him water?

I don't know why I kept thinking the worst about everything, but my brain just kept focusing on the bad stuff. Like when I tried to remember some of our happy times together, my mind dredged up that awful morning when I'd snatched Skelly's Cheerios away. In fact, that's probably why—in my dream—he was wandering around all thirsty. Right before he stumbled into the desert, I'd probably snatched his milk away.

"Jake?"

I heard my mother come into the room. I stayed still and pretended to be asleep.

Ma didn't fall for it. She pulled the afghan away like it was a magician's cloth.

I opened one eye.

Standing in the doorway was another cop. A different cop than the one who I'd ridden with on Wednesday. This one was young and in good shape. He was holding a helmet in his hand, so I knew he was a bike cop.

It looked like there was something in his other hand, too. But the doorway was blocking it from my view.

"Jake, this is Officer Rios," my mother said. "He was just over at the park, and he's got some news for us."

The cop walked the rest of the way into the room.

When I saw his other hand, my blood went cold.

He was holding a white painter's hat.

"Oh, Jesus. No."

Ma rushed over. "No, Jake. Oh, no. It's not what you're thinking. Nothing has happened to Skelly. They found this hat at the park yesterday afternoon. But they think it's good news, Jake. They think it's a *lead*. It means that Skelly's probably been there.

"Yesterday, right?" she asked Officer Rios. "You think he was there yesterday."

He hemmed and hawed a little. "Well, we think it's possible he was there yesterday. Like I already told you, ma'am, my partner and I found the hat at the edge of the lake around four thirty P.M. But we have no way of telling exactly when it got there."

My brain froze around his words.

At the edge of the lake.

From that second on, the rest of what he said faded in and out. There was something about how the hat had been near the water, but not in it. And something else about how there was no evidence of foul play.

Finally, he started backing toward the hall. "So mainly, I just wanted to come by and tell you folks that the search we're going to do today is pretty routine. And that we're very confident that we're not going to find anything down there. But, well . . . just to be sure . . ."

He lowered his voice.

". . . we've sent down a couple of divers."

Ma's hand flew over her mouth.

Right away, Officer Rios started going on and on about how he'd seen lots of these water searches. And how they almost never found anything. And how he'd come back to give us an update as soon as he could.

But Ma didn't nod. Didn't walk him to the door. Didn't do anything.

After he left, I called Aunt Marguerite. She and James were at our house in fifteen minutes. Mrs. Russell came running in behind them.

Officer Rios had left the painter's hat on the coffee table. It's weird, too, how totally different their reactions were when they saw it there.

James mouthed a silent cuss word.

Aunt Marguerite glued her eyes to it and kept them there all the way to her seat.

Mrs. Russell put it on.

I'm not kidding. She snatched it off the table, stuck it on her head, and said it wasn't coming off until Skelly got home.

Ma smiled slightly.

After that, the tension eased in the room a little, and I turned on the TV just for the noise. A baseball game was on, but I doubt if any of us could have told you who was playing. The TV screen was just a place to aim our eyes while we waited.

Three times I tried changing rooms. Once I went into the kitchen and made paper airplanes out of the napkins in the holder. The other two times, I went to my room and rolled around on my bed. But it was never long before I was back in the living room with the others.

Aunt Marguerite was the first one to spot Officer Rios coming up the front-porch steps. "Ohmigod, he's back."

She leaped from her chair and took off running.

James was right on her heels.

Ma was on his.

When the dust finally settled, Mrs. Russell and I were the only ones who hadn't moved a muscle. She glanced over at me. "If the news is good, it'll get here quick enough. If the news is bad, I ain't in no hurry."

I turned my eyes away from the window. Everyone was on the porch, and I couldn't stand to watch.

Seconds passed.

Then, suddenly, there was a bang. I looked over and saw James's meaty face pressed against the pane in a wild grin.

"THEY . . . DIDN'T . . . FIND . . . HIM!"

I thought my heart was going to explode. I sprang off the couch and started jumping up and down. "They didn't find him! They didn't find him! Did you hear that, Mrs. Russell? I knew he was okay! I knew it! I knew it!"

I grabbed the painter's hat off her head and put it on mine.

"This stupid hat isn't even his, I bet! And even if it was his, there are a million ways it could have gotten to the edge of the water. Like the wind could have blown it. Or a dog might have carried it down there. Or—"

"OR A WHOOPING CRANE COULD HAVE FLOWN IT!" she shrieked.

I stopped jumping and just stood there. I mean, that's the whole trouble with Mrs. Russell. Just when you think that you may have made a connection, she goes and says something so freaky it scares you.

Seconds later, my mother came running into the room. She pulled Mrs. Russell up from her chair and hugged us both.

"Oh, Jake, thank God. Oh, Alma, they didn't find him!"

She took our hands and pulled us into the kitchen. Aunt Marguerite had already started making sandwiches. "Who's hungry?" she asked us.

97

We all shouted, "I am," like a bunch of three-year-olds.

It seems odd, I guess, that our happiest moment in days would be *not* finding Skelly. But when your week is as stressful as ours had been, you don't really sit around and analyze whether it's okay to feel good for a second and eat a peanut butter sandwich.

James and I took our lunch outside and ate it on the porch. We didn't talk much. Just sat on the top step, chewed, and swallowed.

I was standing up to take my plate inside when I saw a cab turn down the street. James saw it, too.

We both craned our necks. There was something weird strapped to the top of the roof. Something metal, it looked like.

"What the heck?" said James.

The cab got closer.

James squinted. "Is that what I think it is? Does that guy actually have a—"

"Grocery cart," I said in amazement. "He's got a grocery cart strapped to his cab."

The car slowed down and began inching past the Waxmans'.

James started talking out the side of his mouth. "Ten to one, that guy stole that cart."

I looked at him oddly. "He can't hear you, James. He's in the car, one house over."

But James kept talking in that same stupid way. "Yeah, well all I'm saying is that those carts are worth a lot of money, that's all."

Just then, the car swung over to the curb and the driver got out. He started walking toward James and me.

He was muscular, with a tattoo.

James stopped moving his lips completely and began talking like a ventriloquist. "What's he coming over here for? What does he want with us? Tell him we don't live here."

By now, the man was almost to the porch. I was thinking that maybe I should go get Ma, when I heard the front door open behind me.

"Yes? Can I help you?" Ma called out.

The driver shrugged. "I don't know, I hope so. I'm looking for 433 Eighth Avenue," he said. "I thought it was next door, but I couldn't find a house number."

Ma hesitated a second, then pointed to the small 4-3-3 over our door.

"Well, this is the right address," she told him. "But no one here called a taxi."

In a flash, the driver spun around and headed back to his cab.

"Wait! Hold it! Don't move!" he hollered.

He opened the back door of the car and reached in with both arms.

Carefully, he helped his passenger into the street.

Ma started to sob.

Skelly was home.

We whooped it up like you wouldn't believe. Laughing and hollering and jumping all around in the street.

Skelly seemed confused by the attention. But when his eyes finally focused on my mother, his whole face lit up.

"Hullo, you sweetie pie," he said.

Ma put her arms around him and held on tight. He was sweaty and dirty, and his face was full of gray whiskers. And to me, he never looked greater.

The cab driver, whose name turned out to be Campbell Burns, stood back and watched it all happen. He was patient and quiet. But when the celebration finally ended and Ma invited him inside, he sat down and told us what he knew.

He was stopped at a light in a not-so-good part of the city, when a grocery cart came rolling off the sidewalk and almost sideswiped his cab.

"At first, I thought it had rolled off the curb by itself," he said. "But when I pulled over to get it out of the street, this nice old gentleman came around the corner, stepped down off the curb, and started pushing it."

Campbell shook his head. "Luckily, it wasn't a busy street. He was down there near some old abandoned warehouses. So I figured he was probably a homeless guy. But when I got back in my cab, there was something about him that just didn't add up."

He pointed. "For one thing, that's a pretty decent haircut he's got there. And his shoes were so clean they looked almost new. Also, most homeless guys I've seen don't push around shopping carts that are empty. So I decided to go over and talk to him a minute. And that's when I spotted his ID necklace, with his address."

He smiled a little. "He got kinda stubborn when I tried to get him in the cab, though. Wouldn't come without that damned cart of his. So I figured, what the heck, and I tied it to the roof."

At this point, Mrs. Russell became so overwhelmed with gratitude that she rushed to his chair and hugged his neck.

"God love you, Candle Burns!" she hollered.

Ma pulled her off the best she could. *"Campbell,"* she said. "His name is *Campbell,* Alma."

"Why?" squealed Mrs. Russell. "Is he full of soup? HA!"

Campbell grinned again, and said he had to get back to work.

I went back outside to help him get the grocery cart off of his car. I stalled around a minute, then finally came out with it.

"Campbell? You think he's okay, don't you?"

"Okay?"

"Yeah. I mean, I know he needs a shower and a shave and all. But besides that kind of stuff, you think Skelly's okay, right? Like you don't think anyone . . . *hurt* him."

Campbell stopped what he was doing and looked down at me. "Well, he should definitely be checked out by a doctor. But from what I saw, your grandpop seemed to be in pretty decent shape. In fact, until we had that little problem about not leaving his cart, he didn't even seem in a particularly bad mood."

As we were talking, Campbell Burns glanced in the back window of his cab. Then he opened the door and reached inside again.

"I'll tell you one good thing, though," he said. "Wherever he wandered off to, he must have run into a kind soul along the way, because someone saw to it that he had water."

He handed me a large plastic bottle. "I gave him more, but he drank it on the way home."

When I came inside, I stood the empty bottle on my grandfather's nightstand. As a memento, I guess you'd call it.

Before he went to bed that night, he filled it with water and put it in his closet next to the soup.

12

Graduation Boy

We put the cart in his room.

We're not going to leave it there forever, Ma says. Just for a while.

For three days after he got home, Skelly slept all night and napped all day. In between the sleeping and napping, my mother fixed all his favorite meals.

On Monday, Dr. Bloomfield said he checked out fine.

To me, though, one of the most surprising things about Skelly's great adventure was how fast our family went back to our usual routines. I mean, after an ordeal like that, you'd think that a family would be changed in some huge, drastic way. Like everyone would go around humming and smiling and appreciating all the little things in life, for instance.

And you'd *especially* think, that the very next Sunday at Family Night dinner, the cousin who is in high school would not stick his thumb in another family member's mashed potatoes.

Only he did.

And even though James didn't lick it first this time, I still don't consider that a monumental leap in our relationship.

I have to admit, though, there was one thing that James did that night that shocked me like you wouldn't believe. After dinner, when Aunt Marguerite got my grandfather ready for his walk, James went into Skelly's room and came out with the grocery cart. He said he thought Skelly might like to "take it for a spin."

Right away, Aunt Marguerite started shaking her head. "Oh, no. We're not taking that cart with us, James. No way."

But James just smiled and said, "Way." And before she could give him another argument, he carried the cart down the front-porch steps to the sidewalk.

He and Skelly started to push. For the first time ever, I sat on the front steps and waited for them to come back. I was sure that James would never go through with it. I mean, in spite of his many personality disorders, James has always been popular at school. So I was positive that as soon as he got on a busy street, it would occur to him that he looked like a dork and he'd bail.

But as amazing as this sounds, thirty minutes later, when they came around the corner again, James was still walking next to Skelly, pushing that cart like it was the most natural thing in the world.

And so that's how my family was changed by my grandfather's ordeal, I guess. Not in huge, drastic ways. Not even in our relationships with one another. But in personal little ways that didn't make much noise.

As for me, before he got lost, I had pretty much made

up my mind that I wasn't inviting Skelly to graduation. Especially not after the restaurant incident. The risk just seemed too big.

But on the afternoon that Campbell Burns brought him home, I sat on the edge of his bed as he was lying down for a nap, and I put an invitation in his hand.

He looked at the front, then turned it over.

"What's this?"

"It's an invitation to my graduation, Skell. I want you to come, okay? I mean, it's pretty important for you to be there, don't you think? Even if you don't remember, at least I'll always know that you saw me get my diploma."

Skelly examined it again.

"What this?" he asked.

I stood up and smiled. "Oh, no you don't. You can't get out of it that easy. You're coming, Skell. Next Saturday night, we've got a date to my graduation. Okay?"

He nodded.

"Excellent," I told him. Then I hugged him for a second and left.

When I got to the hall, I heard him mumble, "What's this?"

Graduation was at seven o'clock Saturday night in the school gym.

On Friday afternoon, the gym had still looked like a gym. I mean, the stage had been set up so we could practice going up and getting our diplomas and all. But the teachers and custodians weren't even close to having everything ready.

Behind the stage, half of a banner was partially tacked to the gym wall. If you turned your head sideways, you could read the slogan, which was the "theme," I guess you'd call it. It said:

CLIMB THE LEARNING LADDER OF SUCCESS.

READ, READ, READ!

All that morning, teachers had kept trying to balance tall piles of books on top of these brightly colored red-and-yellow ladders. But the first time someone clomped too heavily across the stage, the books would come crashing to the floor.

In between the crashing books, the custodians were pulling out the bleachers on each side of the gym for the audience and setting up chairs for the graduates, who would sit in the middle.

Since my class has more than five hundred kids in it, we'd spent almost half a day on Thursday just trying to line ourselves up in alphabetical order.

It's amazing how complicated the ABC's can get when five hundred eighth graders are involved. Finally, one of the teachers got so frustrated, she made everyone memorize the names of the two people directly in front of us, and the two people behind us in line. Then all day long, she would suddenly turn and point to kids at random, and they'd have to yell out the names of their group, in order. Like every few minutes you'd hear some poor kid shouting, "FARKLE, FARLEY, FARNSIE, FARROW, FASSEE!" Or "BUBBY, BUCKLE, BUDSY, BUFFERS, BUGDORF!"

Lucas Carney's was the stupidest, I thought: CAAR,

CAR, CARNEY, CARR, CARRH. When he said it, it sounded like he was stuttering. Me and Lucas hadn't seen each other for a while. But we ended up laughing about that.

My own group was Monk, Moolicker, Moon, Mudder, Mulrooney. I hadn't known Ricky Moolicker before graduation practice. But he turned out to be a pretty good guy, and the two of us messed around a lot.

Anyhow, on Saturday night before the ceremony, I finally started getting sort of excited about the whole thing. I must have tied my tie about twenty times before I got it exactly right. I think I went a little overboard on the hair gel, too. I don't know why, but the big events of your life just seem to require a little extra hold.

All together I had given out five invitations: Ma, Skelly, Aunt Marguerite, James, and Mrs. Russell.

Mrs. Russell was my mother's idea. She used the old "Mrs. Russell loves you like a grandson" routine on me. But the truth is, I'd been planning to invite her anyway. After all, it wasn't like I was going to have to sit next to her at the ceremony. And even though she'd be wearing a nurse's uniform, white is a popular color at graduation, so I figured she'd probably blend in with the normal people okay.

At least that's what I thought before we picked her up that night.

With Skelly in the backseat, my mother and I drove over to Mrs. Russell's house around six o'clock. We had just pulled up at the curb when she came out her front door.

She was wearing a small mixing bowl on her head.

I closed my eyes. "No," I groaned. "No, no, no."

Ma leaned down and looked through my window. "Good Lord in heaven," she said.

By this time Mrs. Russell was already at the car. But instead of getting right in the backseat, she bent down next to the window and banged on the glass with her knuckles.

"Yoo-hoo! Hello, graduation boy!"

I turned and looked at my mother. "Please. Just get a gun and shoot me."

Finally, Mrs. Russell opened the back door and slid in next to Skelly.

"Hello, Skelly, you big handsome fella," she said, giving him a hug.

After that, she tapped on my head. "Well? Who's going to be the first one to compliment me on my new nurse's cap? I ordered it from the catalog especially for this occasion. It just came this morning. Isn't it cute? It's called a pillbox. Get it? HA!"

Ma smiled. "It's wonderful, Alma. Very stylish. Jake and I were just commenting on it. It's charming, isn't it, Jake?"

I made a noise and slumped lower in my seat. Maybe if I stayed below window level, no one would see me.

Unfortunately, after picking up Mrs. Russell, there was still one more stop to make. Earlier, Aunt Marguerite had called from work and said she'd be a little late, so she wanted us to pick up James.

When we drove up his street, he was sitting in the yard waiting for us. He was wearing cut-off jeans and a T-shirt with the sleeves ripped out, and was eating a corn dog. Also, since the last time I'd seen him, he'd gotten a nose ring.

As soon as he opened the door, I looked over the seat at him.

"You understand that we're not on our way to Wrestle-mania. Correct?" I said.

James faked a grin. There was corn dog on his tooth.

By the time we pulled into the school parking lot, I was so far down in my seat, I was on the floor almost.

As soon as Ma stopped the car, I bailed right out and headed for the gym.

"Jake! Wait! Don't I get a kiss?" she called.

I froze in my tracks. Great way to start things off. Your mother hollering for a smooch across a crowded parking lot.

I sprinted back, pecked her on the cheek, and ran off again. When I was a safe enough distance away, I slowed to a stop and looked back.

Ma was helping Skelly out of the car. He was wearing his brand-new suit from Sears. And his new red clip-on bow tie. He look distinguished, almost. Like a retired doc-tor or a college professor.

I watched from the sidewalk as Ma combed, and then recombed, his hair. Skelly held his head perfectly still while she made his part.

After she finished, she put her hand real gentle on his

cheek. She must have told him how handsome he was, because he started to beam.

I smiled a little and walked on.

We'd gotten there in plenty of time for my mother to find seats near the door. It was important for her to be close to an exit in case Skelly got restless.

In the meantime I hung out with a bunch of other kids who were early like me. It wasn't long, though, before the teachers started rounding us up to get in line.

Like a lot of gyms, ours is a big, square room with a door in each corner. Mrs. Rook, our school principal, had drilled it into our heads that when we walked in, we should keep the pace slow and dignified.

"Walk in time to the music." She must have told us that a million times. "We do not *dance* in time to the music. Or *stroll* in time to the music. Or *mosey* or *march* or *strut* in time to the music."

She stopped here and searched the gym until she found Jerome Sheridan.

She raised her voice a level. "And above all, Jerome, my pet, we do not *get down* in time to the music!"

Everybody laughed. But it wasn't until the music started for real that night, that I finally understood why she'd been so insistent. Graduation music sounds almost like church music when it's playing for real, so you don't really want a bunch of yahoos mucking up the mood.

When I started into the gym, my stomach was flip-flopping like you wouldn't believe. I kept my head down and concentrated on the backs of Ricky Moolicker's shoes.

Somehow, I got to my seat without tripping. I relaxed a little then and looked in the bleachers for Ma. I stretched my neck every way I could, but there were too many heads in the way to see the bleachers near the door, so finally I gave up trying. Maybe it was even better like this. Maybe if I couldn't see Skelly, I wouldn't be as nervous about him.

Anyhow, it took a while for everyone to get settled. But at last Mrs. Rook, who was sitting with the other speakers onstage, stepped up to the microphone and began her "Welcome to Graduation" speech.

Like with every principal I've ever known, whenever Mrs. Rook starts to talk, she promises not to blabber on forever, and then she blabbers on forever.

Not only that, but at graduation ceremonies, one blabberer is never enough. Like the man who came after Mrs. Rook—some state senator or somebody—talked twice as long as she did. And according to the program, we still hadn't gotten to the official "Greetings from the President of the Board of Education."

I sank down in my chair and closed my eyes.

Ricky gave me an elbow in the ribs. "Hey, Moon, what time is it?"

I held up my watch so he could see. Seven forty-five.

He rolled his head back in annoyance. "Geez, when is this guy going to button it up? My baby brother is never going to last."

I shifted in my seat and wondered about Skelly.

Finally, the president of the Board of Education stepped up to the microphone. He wanted to bid us a "warm and gracious good evening," he said.

Ricky Moolicker groaned. "A warm and gracious get off the stage," he grumbled back.

I closed my eyes again and tried to relax.

Unfortunately—even though I didn't know it at the time—at the other end of the gym, Ma was still waiting for Aunt Marguerite to show up. My aunt had said that she would be there by seven-fifteen "at the latest," so by now my mother had started to panic.

In her alarm, Ma sent Mrs. Russell outside to look for Marguerite.

You understood that part, right? Ma sent *Mrs. Russell* on a search mission.

And so, what do you know. Within minutes, Mrs. Russell was missing, too.

Now, here's where the story really starts to get lively. My mother finally decided that she had no choice but to go find both of them. So she put James in charge of Skelly.

James. The corn dog with the nose ring.

And who knows, maybe it might even have worked out. Except that right after Ma left the gym, James spotted Aunt Marguerite on the other side of the room. So my brilliant cousin told Skelly to "stay put." And then he ran out the door, raced to the other side of the building, hollered to his mother to follow him, and then ran back to Skelly as fast as he could.

But *surprise.*

Skelly was already gone.

Or at least James *thought* he was gone. Only here comes another one of those twists I mentioned before.

Because, except for James, everyone in the gymnasium knew *exactly* where Skelly was.

Or as Ricky Moolicker put it when he nudged me in the ribs again, "Who's the old guy walking up the steps?"

My stomach heaved.

When I looked up, Skelly had already reached the top of the stairs.

Mrs. Rook nodded at him and smiled. She later admitted that she thought he was some retired bigwig sent from the superintendent's office who was looking for his seat. So, as my grandfather carefully made his way around the chairs of dignitaries, no one said a word.

Not even when he headed for the red-and-yellow paint ladders.

I bent over in my chair and prayed. Jesus, Ma, Jesus. Please . . . just . . . *see* . . . him.

The crash came next.

Skelly had tried to lift one of the ladders, and the books had fallen onto the floor.

"Uh-oh! Uh-oh!" he yelled out.

Instantly, two security guards rushed up the stairs and grabbed him.

Skelly hollered in surprise. He raised his head then and saw the audience. I honestly don't think that until that very moment, he'd even been aware they were there.

Seconds later, my grandfather hid his head in the

sleeve of his new suit from Sears. And he started to cry.

I still don't remember running onto the stage that night. I do remember tripping when I went up the steps. But somehow I caught myself and kept going.

Skelly heard the noise and looked over.

I slowed down and forced myself to walk. "Shh, Skelly. Shh. It's okay. I promise it is. Everything is fine."

Skelly looked at my face. He didn't have a clue.

"Come on, Skell. You know me. Don't let the hair gel fool you, okay? Look at my face again. See? It's me. It's . . ."

I paused.

". . . it's Claude Harper."

As soon as he heard the name, his shoulders relaxed a little. "Claude Harper?" he repeated softly.

By then, I was right next to him. I put my arm around his waist. "Yeah, Skell. It's Claude. And here's what I'm thinking, okay? I'm thinking that maybe you and I should go right over there to those steps. See them over there?"

I pointed. "What do you say? Hmm? You want to walk over to those steps with me?"

I kept my arm around his waist, and the two of us started to walk. His feet shuffled heavily, as if he was suddenly tired. We took it slow.

When we got to the end of the stage, Ma and Aunt Marguerite were waiting at the bottom of the stairs.

Skelly and I went carefully down.

They took his hands and led him away.

* * *

I got my diploma a little while later. The walk to the stage was tougher the second time. I kept my eyes glued on Ricky's shoes again and tried to block out the whispers.

When Mrs. Rook finally called my name, James whistled so loud from the audience, she laughed. As she handed me my diploma, she shook my hand and held it extra long. She said I should be proud.

After that, I walked down the steps and out the gym door, and kept going till I got to the car.

The door was locked, but the rest of them were there within minutes.

I hugged Ma first, then everyone else except James.

We'd talk about this later. And forever, probably. But right now I just wanted to go home.

I got in the backseat. Skelly slid in beside me and I held his hand.

As Ma pulled out of the parking lot, I rolled down the window and breathed in the cool air. My shoulders loosened up a little.

Next to me, Skelly sighed.

I smiled at him in the dark and looked out into the night sky.

In my mind, I could almost hear him whisper, "Atta boy, Jake. Atta boy."

For more information on Alzheimer's you can contact the national office by mail or phone at:

Alzheimer's Association National Office
919 North Michigan Avenue, Suite 1000
Chicago, Illinois 60611-1676
(800) 272-3900
(312) 335-8700
Fax: (312) 335-1110

To locate the chapter nearest you, call
(800) 272-3900.
Further information can be found on their web site at:
www.alz.org

You can also visit these web sites:

www.mayohealth.org
www.mediconsult.com
www.onhealth.com

Don't miss these favorites from Newbery Medalist

CYNTHIA VOIGT

"Entertaining, interesting,
and well-written."
—*New York Times Book Review*
WINNER OF THE
EDGAR ALLAN POE AWARD

"Beautifully written . . .
miraculously convincing and
moving."—*Publishers Weekly*

"Enjoy this one for the
pure pleasure of the creepy
goings-on."—*Booklist*